Home
Is the North

Also by Walt Morey
GENTLE BEN

Home
Is the North

by
Walt Morey

*Best wishes
from
Walt Morey*

ILLUSTRATED BY
ROBERT SHORE

E. P. Dutton & Co., Inc.

New York

This book is for the women in my life, Trudy and Rosalind, my mother and my wife.

List of Illustrations

.

one

For two weeks the boy had circled each day on the calendar. This last one had dropped him into a gloom so deep he was not aware the fire had gone out in the stove and the woodbox was empty. Both were unforgivable sins in Alaska in winter.

He was aware only of the brutal voice of the storm, the eternal slamming of icy blasts against the cabin's stout walls, and the knowledge that the snow was growing deeper.

He didn't even notice when Mickie, his big wolflike Malamute dog, lifted his head from where he lay before the cold stove, cocked his sharp ears toward the door, and listened intently. After a little while Mickie rose, clicked across the floor, reared his front paws against the window sill, and began to whine. Only then did the boy rouse. "What living thing could be abroad in such weather?" Curious, he went to the window, scraped frost from the glass with a fingernail, and peered out.

Through the driving snow he made out the shape of a

strange white boat tying up at the little dock. A moment later two men jumped ashore. With shoulders hunched against the lash of the storm, they plowed up the narrow trail toward the cabin. The boy recognized Captain Ed Bishop and his deck hand, Big George. These men had stopped often in the past, as Alaskans do, to say "hello" and ask if there was anything they could do to help him and his grandmother. They lived alone out here fifty miles from their nearest neighbor and a hundred miles from Orca City.

The boy swung the door wide. The men stumbled in with a gush of wind and snow, and he slammed the door again. They shook snow from their parkas and shoved back the hoods. Captain Ed gave him a big white grin and said: "Hello, Brad. Haven't seen you in a month of Sundays. How're you folks making out in this storm?"

"All right." Mickie crowded against Brad's legs, and the boy reached down automatically to put a hand on the big wolflike head. "I didn't know you at first. You got a new boat?"

"New to us," Big George said proudly. "She's a real humdinger! The Skipper just bought her in Ketchikan. We're on our way home."

Brad liked them both. They were friendly and had been considerate of his grandmother. They were big, but in different ways. Captain Ed Bishop was dark, with snapping black eyes and a crown of curly hair as black as a crow's wings. He was tall and lean-muscled, with bony features and a long jaw. His shoulders were wide, his chest flat. He carried himself proudly, his dark head high.

Big George was blond, with straight hair so thin on top his

pink scalp peeked through. His legs were long and straight, and a great breadth of chest and shoulders stretched taut the buttons on his blue woolen shirt. His face was broad, scar-furrowed, and topped by blond lumpy brows. One ear was as thick as a muffin. A cauliflower ear, Brad's father had called it, caused by being struck too often by a fist. Big George had once been a prize fighter. For all his size his step was light and quick. His big head was thrust slightly forward, as if he measured an opponent for a bone-shattering charge. He was pleasantly ugly until he smiled. Then you knew that here was a gentle, kindly man, but one who could be as dangerous as a goaded bear if once aroused.

Captain Ed asked, "Where's your grandmother, Brad?"

Brad concentrated on patting the thick fur between Mickie's golden almond eyes, and did not answer.

Captain Ed became conscious then of the chill in the room, the cold stove. He glanced about. Unwashed dishes were piled in the sink. The table still held breakfast dishes, and some, he guessed, from last night. There was a pair of unwashed frying pans on the back of the stove, along with a pot half full of some sort of cooked cereal. He looked at the boy again and asked: "Anything wrong, Brad? Is your grand-mother all right?"

Brad scratched at the base of Mickie's ears, and Mickie twisted his big head to get the full benefit. Finally Brad looked up into Captain Ed's face and said in a flat voice, "She's dead."

For a little, both men just looked at him. They saw a slim, sober boy with a thatch of straight brown hair and gray eyes that were dark with the strain of the past two weeks. His shoulders were square and bony, his arms long and thin, the wrists sticking out of sleeves that were too short.

A fresh gust of wind moaned around the corners of the cabin, and against the frosted windowpane shadows of snowflakes slid like wing-shot birds down to the sill. Captain Ed finally scrubbed a big hand across his mouth and said gently, "You want to tell us about it, Brad?"

Brad continued to scratch Mickie's ears. He couldn't meet Captain Ed's black eyes just then. He had to fight down the tears before he could talk. Finally he said: "It was two weeks ago. Mickie and I went down the beach for a hike. We were gone a couple of hours. When—when we got back she was lying here on the floor. At first I thought she had fainted. After a while I knew she hadn't. I don't know what happened."

Captain Ed, speaking more to George than to Brad, said: "She had a heart condition for years. I'd guess she had an attack." He added quietly to Brad: "You were all alone? You—didn't have anybody?"

"Just Mickie and me. I—I took her up to that crevice back of the cabin on the sled. I made a big pile of rocks over her like the Indians used to do."

Captain Ed sat down in the nearest chair. He exchanged looks with George. Finally he asked, "You got anybody else?"

"An Aunt Clara Haskin in Seattle, Mom's sister."

"What about her?"

Brad shrugged. His eyes dropped to Mickie sitting beside

"Just Mickie and me."

14

him. "Gram wrote her last year when my folks drowned off Kodiak. Nothing came of it. I guess she wasn't much interested. Maybe because Gram wasn't related to her. She was Dad's mother."

He knew that wasn't true. Aunt Clara had been keenly interested in Brad's future long before his parents drowned. He remembered his parents discussing Aunt Clara's letters several years ago, and his mother had sounded annoyed. "Clara's a good teacher, but when she starts on one of her crusades you have to slap her down hard to stop her. Well, she's not telling me how to raise Brad. We're not sending him two thousand miles away to school at his age. Why, he'd be frightened to death in a big city and in a big school. He'd be a total stranger with not one friend to cling to. When he's ready for high school will be soon enough to think of sending him so far from home."

"What'll you do?" his father had asked.

"I'll go right on doing the same thing. I've taken Brad through the first five grades myself. I can take him through the next three. If Clara wants to help with advice, I'll appreciate it."

Brad had to admit Aunt Clara had been very helpful. Each year she had laid out a whole course of study that his mother had followed. And she'd been generous with all sorts of books. There had been regular hours of school, and even examinations. He'd finished the eighth grade just weeks before his parents drowned off Kodiak Island.

Gram wrote to Aunt Clara of the tragedy, and again the letters began to fly. Aunt Clara wanted to come up and get Brad immediately. He was ready for high school now, her letters insisted. He should have proper guidance, and the benefits of city schools.

Gram was about to give in. She was old and not too strong, and Aunt Clara's letters were demanding.

But Brad had argued, too. "This is my home. I don't want to go to some big-city school in the States. Mom said I didn't have to, not yet. Remember? Let me stay here with you this year. You can't live out here alone. Then next year, if I have to go to school in the States maybe you can go with me. Write Aunt Clara a tough letter, Gram. Tell her that's what we're going to do. Mom said she'll back off if you stand up to her." He had finally talked her into writing the letter.

Aunt Clara's answer accepted the arrangement: "Very well, I guess a year off from school at his age won't hurt Brad. But next year you'll have to make some decision about him. After all, he can't grow up a heathen. I hope you understand my interest in Brad, Jesse. He is my sister's child, and now that she's gone, the only relative I have in the world."

"Clara's right," Gram had said. "Next year we've got to do something. But I guess it's all right for you to stay out of school this year."

He had almost told Captain Ed there was no relative. But he remembered just in time that Gram might have mentioned his Aunt Clara on one of his visits. It was best to admit her existence, then try to turn attention from her. Apparently it worked, for Captain Ed now asked:

"What do you figure to do?"

Gram was gone. Now he could make his own decision. "I'm staying here," he said, trying to bring a confidence to his voice he didn't feel. "This is home. Mine and Mickie's."

18

"Just the two of you?"

"We'll make out."

"You have, so far. Your grandmother was a great one for canning and curing food. You've probably got enough to last all winter. What'll you do when it gives out?"

"Get more. When fishing season opens, maybe I'll go to work in a cannery or on board a seiner. I'm big and strong enough. I can earn what we need."

Captain Ed nodded his dark head soberly. "I guess you could at that."

"You don't think it'll get too lonesome living out here alone?" Big George asked.

"We've made it so far. When the storm lets up and we can get outside again, it'll be better."

Captain Ed and George exchanged looks. Captain Ed observed, "You seem to have things pretty well planned out." He stood up as if about to leave, then added as an afterthought, "As long as we're here and you can't do anything during the storm, why not come home with us for a few days?"

"I don't know," Brad considered. "I hadn't thought about going anyplace." After the first few days he'd thought of nothing else. He was lonesome, achingly, desperately lonesome. He wanted to be around people again, have someone to talk to. He'd have gone crazy without Mickie, but Mickie couldn't take the place of a human. Brad had heard stories about cabin fever, a form of madness brought on by being alone too long. It usually happened to lonely prospectors, miners, and trappers. It could happen to him. But he didn't want to appear anxious.

19

"That's a good idea," George urged, glancing about the room that was now becoming uncomfortably cool. "It'd break the monotony for us, too. Being alone is fine most of the year. But not in winter. You come along. The change'll be good for all of us."

"That's the truth," Captain Ed agreed.

"How'd I get back?" Brad asked, trying to act as if he were holding out to the last.

"We'll bring you whenever you like."

"That's about fifty miles. A hundred, round trip." Brad knew it was expensive to operate a boat the size of the one they'd come in.

"We need a few shakedown cruises to get the feel of the *Annie B*," Captain Ed explained. "Every boat has its peculiarities. We want to know the *Annie B*'s before seining time. We can just as well cruise this way."

Brad didn't know boats had peculiarities, but if Captain Ed said so, it must be. He could think of no other arguments, and he hoped he'd held out long enough so they wouldn't guess how much he wanted to go. "Maybe for a few days, then," he said.

"Come on, Champ." George grinned. "I'll help you toss some clothes in a sack while the Skipper looks over the house and makes sure everything's locked up and battened down."

Brad had a sudden thought. "I can't leave Mickie. Will it be all right to take him?"

"Sure." Captain Ed leaned forward and patted Mickie's wolflike head. "We had five dogs once, a sled team. They're all dead now. Our lead dog, Bobby, was the spitting image of Mickie. Annie'll be tickled to see him. She loved Bob. It'll be a little like old times for her. You and George get your duds. I'll lock up."

Captain Ed's wife was known throughout the Territory as Stampede Annie. Brad had seen her once, a year ago, when she had stopped with Captain Ed. He had heard many stories about her. She was a product of the gold-rush days, a dead shot. She ran her own trap line, had been a top dog-team woman, could skin and cut up game faster than most men. The rugged, virgin country and brutal climate had used her hard. She was small-boned and thin, almost scrawny, with weather-burned hands and face, and bright blue eyes as sharp as an eagle's. She looked tough and leathery. Her straight black hair, dusted with gray at the temples, was pulled tight around her small head and fastened in a roll at the back of her neck. Brad guessed she was older than his mother but younger than Gram. About halfway between. About fifty, he decided. But her movements, as she hurried about getting supper, were quick, and there was a birdlike alertness about her that made her seem years younger.

Now Brad stood in the center of Annie's warm kitchen and looked around while Captain Ed explained how he happened to be here.

The kitchen was like the one at home, big and roomy because that's where the family mostly lived in winter. There was a table in one corner, with a wood stove in the other, and numerous open shelves and cupboards lining the walls. A window with green potted plants on the sill overlooked the back porch that was piled high with ricks of wood. The big difference was the gunrack, nailed high on one wall. There were four guns in the rack, all shiny and oiled. The top one

21

was a heavy rifle, a magnificent gun with telescopic sights and beautiful lines. The next was a shotgun; a third, he guessed, a light rifle. He could not identify the bottom gun. It was small and neat, too small for a rifle or shotgun.

Brad carried his clothes in an old bed sheet George had made into a hamper by drawing up the four corners and tying them.

Mickie sat on his tail beside Brad, tongue hanging out and black nostrils twitching. Brad was smelling the same wonderful odors, the delicious mouth-watering aroma of food cooking in the pots and pans on the stove. He'd almost forgotten how exciting those smells were. Mickie and he had been living mostly on canned food. He'd tried cooking, but the steak burned, the roast never did get done, and even Mickie couldn't eat the biscuits.

Annie said in a voice that startled him with its depth and rough, gravelly quality: "I'm sorry about your grandmother, son. She was a real nice person." Then she looked at Mickie, and Brad had the odd feeling that she forgot all else. "Bobby! old Bobby!" Her deep voice was amazingly soft and gentle. Her small hard hand gripped Mickie's muzzle. She tipped his head up and studied his wolflike head intently. "Same look around the eyes, same black markings in the face, broad head, good strong jaws, same gray-white coat." She was talking to herself, her husky voice almost crooning, and Mickie's tail was thumping the floor. "Malamute. Your papa and mama had some wolf in 'em. About a quarter, I'd guess. Good, strong, and tough. And big. About a hundred pounds. Best sled dog in the world. Old Bobby to a tee. What do you know?"

Abruptly she dropped Mickie's muzzle, stepped back, and resolutely folded her hands tightly behind her back. The act squared her narrow shoulders and lifted her small chin. When she spoke, her voice seemed deeper, rougher than ever. "Take him out and put him in Bobby's house. He can't be in here. I won't have a dog in the house. And you'll have to feed and care for him," she told Brad. "I've got other things to do besides fooling with a dog."

"Hey, Annie!" Captain Ed said, surprised. "All five of our dogs were in the house sometimes. Especially Bobby. Remember? What's wrong with Mickie?"

"That's what's wrong," Annie flared. "For years it was dogs, dogs, dogs! I waded through dogs, walked around 'em and fell over 'em fifty times a day. When they got sick I nursed 'em, sat up with 'em, and worried over 'em. When Bobby died I said never again. No more! Now the boy has a dog. That's fine. I'm all for a boy having a dog. But he takes care of him, feeds him, and keeps him out from under my feet. Is that understood?"

"I know it was rough on you," Captain Ed agreed, "especially when Bobby died. We all loved him. But that was more than a year ago. I figured you liked dogs so much you'd be over that and glad to see Mickie."

"Well, I'm not glad to see him," Annie shot back. "Too much is too much."

Brad said hastily: "I'll take care of Mickie. He won't be any trouble to you."

"Good! Take him out and fasten him to Bobby's house. The chain and collar are hanging on the porch. You'll have to keep him tied for a couple of days, till he gets used to it here and won't wander off. And, son"—her rough voice stopped Brad and Mickie at the door. Her small hands were still folded tightly behind her back, her bony chin lifted uncompromisingly—"he is an awful nice dog."

Brad found the chain and collar and buckled the collar around Mickie's neck. Mickie didn't know what to make of it. This was the first collar he'd ever worn. He whined and pawed at the collar and begged Brad with his big golden eyes to take it off. When Brad rose to leave, Mickie lunged against the chain, trying to follow. Brad patted his head reassuringly, and said: "I don't like it either, but I can't help it. We're not home now. So you have to stay out here. It won't hurt you. Malamutes are used to being out in storms much worse than this. This is a good doghouse. And I'll be right inside. It's not your fault she don't like you. She just don't like dogs any more. Maybe if I had to take care of five dogs all at once for years I'd be sick of 'em, too. But don't you worry. We won't stay long. Just a couple of days. Then we'll go back home where we belong, and you can be in the house or anyplace else you want."

When Brad entered the kitchen, Big George had come up from making the *Annie B* snug against the storm.

Annie said to Brad as she whisked back and forth between the table and stove with the dishes: "Ed says you've got an aunt in Seattle. Does she know what happened to you?"

Brad shook his head. "The mail boat hadn't come yet. But she won't be interested. Gram wasn't related to her."

"But she is related to you. She's got to be notified."

"Why? She's clear down in the States, two thousand miles away. I don't mean a thing to her."

24

"She's your aunt, and it's only right she should know," Annie said promptly. "But if it's like you say, there's no big rush. Nobody does anything in winter anyway. So make yourself at home. I'm mighty glad to have you. Now you'd better wash up. Supper's almost ready."

It was the first real cooked meal Brad had eaten in two weeks. There were mashed potatoes and thick brown gravy, a huge venison roast, fluffy sour-dough biscuits hot from the oven, canned peaches, and a big wedge of blueberry pie to top it off.

It was a time Brad knew he would never forget. Snow drove against the kitchen window with silent white fingers, and the voice of the storm came through the sturdy log walls with a low moaning. It was the sort of wild night that drove every animal to seek some sort of shelter to wait its passing. But inside the kitchen it was wonderfully warm and safe. The hurricane lamp hanging from the ceiling lighted every part of the room. There were much talk and banter, as with people who have been long together and know each other well.

Captain Ed observed between mouthfuls, "This's a pretty fair roast, considering."

" 'Considering'! 'Fair'!" Annie was indignant. "Will you listen to the man?" Then she had to tell what had happened on the particular hunt when she got the roast. "I jumped this deer and snapped a shot at him as he started to cross the creek. But he kept right on runnin', so I figured I missed him. But before I can move, another'n runs outa the brush following the first. Well, I let fly at him, too. And you know what?" She glanced around the table while the two men and

Brad waited. "Both them fool deer dropped dead, right in the middle of that creek. And it knee-deep in slush ice. I like to froze to death before I got 'em out. Then I had to dress 'em and pack 'em in. My clothes was crackin' with ice at every step. It's a pure wonder I didn't catch my death of pneumonia or something. 'Fair'? 'Considering'?" she snorted. "You better say that's the best darned roast you ever clamped your teeth onto. It was mighty hard to come by."

Big George kept rubbing the muffin-thick ear, and Brad finally worked up the courage to ask if it bothered him.

"Naw," George said. "It's just habit."

"I'll bet you were a good fighter," Brad said, taking in the breadth of George's chest and shoulders, his scarred face and lumpy brows.

"I wasn't bad," George said modestly. "Almost got a crack at the title once."

"You did?" Brad was impressed.

"That's right. You see, there's this heavyweight they call Cowboy Billy Carter, and the publicity is building up to get him a title shot. Well, my manager worked it around so I get a crack at Carter. We figure if I can beat Carter I'll get the title shot. I can beat anybody I can hang Old Betsy on. That's what I called my right hand. Well, the first round nothing much happens. We look each other over, huntin' a spot to go to work. The second, the fireworks explode. I back that Cowboy into a corner and look for a spot to hang Old Betsy. But before I find it, something hits me. It's like the roof fell in—"

Annie spoiled the finish by producing the punch line: "And when you woke up in the dressing room, your manager

26

said it'd been a great fight. Two punches. He hit you and you hit the floor."

Brad laughed with Annie and Captain Ed.

George scowled; then he laughed, but not quite so loudly as Captain Ed and Annie.

Brad ate until he could scarcely breathe, and still Annie urged more on him. "You're a growing boy," she nagged in her gravelly voice. "You got a lot of filling out to do. How about a little more roast? Nothing like wild meat to stick to a boy's ribs. Then—how about that last piece of pie? It looks about your size. I can guess how you've been eating. A hunk of bread and jelly or a handful of crackers, and you called it a meal. You sure you can't eat that pie?"

He found room for the pie.

When they were finished, Annie heaped a tin plate with scraps from the dinner and said, "Here, son, for your dog."

Brad couldn't help noticing that when she referred to Mickie that impersonal toughness was in her voice again.

He took the plate out to Mickie and squatted in the snow in the protection of the doghouse while Mickie dug eagerly into the pile of food. "I guess you're pretty sick of the grub you've been getting," Brad said. "Me too." He watched Mickie clean the tin to the last crumb without once looking up. Brad patted him again and said: "Sure am glad you're with me. I'd be real lost without you." He stood up to go, and Mickie whined and pulled on the chain. "I can't take you in," Brad explained. "But don't you worry. We'll be back home in a couple of days."

When he returned to the kitchen with the empty tin, the dishes had been washed and put away and the three people

27

were sitting about the cleared table. Annie patted the chair beside her, and Brad sat down.

For a little while he listened to their talk, which was all about the new boat, the *Annie B.* They were excited over her. He gathered that buying the boat had been a big undertaking with all of them.

"She handles like a dream," Captain Ed said.

"You could eat off the deck or the top of the motor, she's that clean," George added.

"And she's solid wood from stem to stern," Captain Ed said. "She'll take anything the Sound can throw at her."

"Wait'll you see the holds," George added enthusiastically. "She'll carry ten thousand salmon easy."

"She'll have to," Annie said soberly. "How much are we in debt for her?"

"Fifteen thousand."

"And we owe it to old Tightfisted Karlson." Annie shook her small head.

"Do you mean Frank Karlson, the man who owns the Orca City Cannery?" Brad suddenly took an interest in the conversation.

"That's the one. You know him, son?" Annie asked.

"No, but Gram did."

"Did she know anything good about him?"

"She didn't like him. She said he'd cheat fishermen on their count if he could, that he was always buying stolen fish from the fish pirates. She blamed him some for my folks getting drowned."

"How was that?"

"There was a poor run in the Sound last year, so Dad and

28

Mother went to Kodiak, where they had a big run. They owed Mr. Karlson money, too. Dad said they had to get it someplace to pay him off because he wouldn't wait. They got caught in that big storm and were drowned."

"And that's the man we're dealing with," Annie said to Captain Ed and George.

"It couldn't be helped," Captain Ed explained. "The bank wouldn't loan us money without plenty of security, and we didn't have it. Only Karlson would take a chance on us."

"Big chance he took," Annie grumbled. "A one-year mortgage on the *Annie B* plus our guarantee to bring him all our catch."

Captain Ed spread his hands in a helpless gesture. "It was that or lose the *Annie B.*"

"I just hope we get to keep her," Annie said darkly.

"All we need is seven or eight good loads and we'll be in the clear," Captain Ed pointed out.

"And the Bureau of Fisheries predicts a big run next season," George added.

"They'd better be right. We're betting everything we've got on it."

"Are you sorry we got the boat?" Captain Ed asked.

Annie shook her head vigorously. "We had to have a new boat. It just scares me thinking of old Karlson holding that sword over our future."

Captain Ed put a big brown hand over Annie's small hard ones. "We'll make out. Don't worry."

Annie's bright blue eyes looked steadily into Captain Ed's black ones. "Sure we will." She smiled suddenly. "I'm just a crepe hanger, I guess."

"When we get Karlson paid off, we'll have the world by the tail on a downhill pull," George said. "And that's a darned good holt."

"The best," Annie agreed, straightening her narrow shoulders. "As soon as the weather clears I want a cruise. It's not every day an old woman like me gets a classy boat like the *Annie B* named after her."

"You'll get it," Captain Ed promised. "Nobody earned the *Annie B* more than you did."

The warmth of the room and the big dinner were having their effect on Brad. He could scarcely hold his head up, and his eyes kept closing in spite of him. Annie noticed, and said, "Come on, son. You're half asleep sitting up."

Carrying a spare lamp, she led him into the other room where a folding cot had been set up. He guessed this was the front room—the living room his mother and Gram would have called it. Annie put the light on the table and said: "This won't be the softest bed in the world, but I guess you won't mind. I could sleep on a gravel pile at your age. I put extra blankets on the chair if you get cold during the night. Sleep as long as you like in the morning."

"This is swell," Brad said. Then he added: "That was an awful good dinner. I guess I was hungrier than I thought."

"Boys usually are." Her small, thin face turned sober. "So you've been batching it alone over there the last two weeks. It can be mighty lonesome alone, especially in winter."

"I had Mickie."

"That's right. I forgot." She reached out suddenly and ruffled his straight brown hair. "Good night, son."

30

The room was cold. Brad undressed in a rush, climbed into his pajamas, blew out the lamp, and jumped into bed.

The coldness of the room and the chill of the covers had knocked the sleep out of him. He was wide awake. He listened to the lonesome moaning of the wind at the cabin's corners. It was a cold, freezing sound. Mickie was out in that. But it wouldn't bother him. His thick coat would turn greater cold than this storm carried. In fact, Mickie was better off outside. Gram had made him stay out. He'd been inside only since they'd been alone.

He listened to the low murmur of voices from the next room. They were talking about the *Annie B* again, dreaming, planning the fishing season a few months ahead. How many times he had lain in bed and listened to his parents and Gram do just that. These were nice people, and it was wonderful being here with them. Out there in the warm friendliness of the kitchen the fierce tensions and aching anxieties that had been building within him the past two weeks had slipped away. A warm and comfortable feeling of belonging and a peace he hadn't known in days flooded over him. He snuggled deeper into the mound of covers as the heat of his body drove the chill away. Drowsiness dragged him downward into sleep. He trailed his hand over the side of the bed, as he'd been doing the past two weeks. But it didn't touch sharp ears and soft warm fur. He felt a faint sense of loss and loneliness. A last conscious thought drifted into his mind. If Annie could just like Mickie, everything would be perfect.

31

two

Brad awoke long before daylight, and for a time he lay there, snug and warm in that half-world between sleeping and waking. Then he remembered where he was, and his eyes flew open and he stared into the room's darkness, seeing nothing. He listened for the sounds of the wind tearing at the corners of the cabin, the moaning of it high in the barren branches of the trees. There was none.

He jumped out of bed, skipped across the cold floor, scratched a trail through the frost on the window, and put his eyes to it. It was dark out. The sky was a midnight blue, but he could see the lacy shapes of the trees, and through them the far-off glitter of stars. It was morning in hours, but the long northern winter dark still lay heavy upon the land. The first hint of dawn was there, but so faint it was a quality of dark that was felt rather than seen. Full dawn, Brad guessed, was at least an hour away. Sometime during the night the storm had blown itself out, and the snow had stopped.

The cold was creeping into him, and he ran back and jumped into bed. The house was quiet. Like all seiners with little to do in winter, they were sleeping in. Brad settled himself in the blankets for another hour's sleep.

But sleep would not come, and he lay staring into the dark. He thought of Captain Ed and Annie and Big George. He pictured again the easy companionship, the fun they'd had at supper, and the good talk afterward. There was the close feeling of family with these three. He remembered his father had once said that George had come to the Bishops' some years ago when Captain Ed had his first boat. He'd stayed with them ever since, not once returning to the States to come back in the spring, as most people who worked the salmon run did. "They're inseparable," his father had said. "The men work together better than most brothers. I'd like to find someone like that to work with me. But a Big George comes along about once in a lifetime."

Brad thought of the positive sound of Annie's deep voice when she'd insisted that Aunt Clara must be notified. She means to do it herself, he thought. He would never change Annie's mind the way he had Gram's, not Stampede Annie's. He didn't know what he was going to do. The one thing he dreaded most was that he might have to leave the North. Near panic threatened to overwhelm him every time he thought of going to a huge, strange city, two thousand miles away, filled with an army of people he'd never seen, and to a school of several thousand students where there was not one friendly or familiar face.

But Annie had said: "There's no big rush. Nobody does anything in the winter anyway." He had time, he told

33

himself, time to think of some way to stop his aunt from taking him away, and time, maybe, even to stop Annie from writing the letter.

There was no use trying to sleep. He'd go out and take Mickie for a run and look around.

He dressed quietly in the dark, made his bed, then tiptoed into the kitchen. The room was still faintly warm. He lighted the lamp and turned up the flame until it barely chased the dark. He lifted a lid off the stove and found that the fire had been banked. Someone would be getting up soon, and it was nice to come into a warm room. He laid a couple of sticks on the coals and cracked the damper. He stopped under the gunrack and looked up at the four guns. That little one at the bottom was just about his size. He'd had such a gun in mind the past three years when he'd begged his father for one. Dad had just kept saying, "We'll see."

It was the big gun at the top that really fascinated him. He pulled a kitchen chair near, stood on the seat, and examined it more closely. It was sleek and heavy and utterly beautiful. He bet it would shoot a mile and kill anything. With such a gun, even a fifteen-year-old boy would be master over any animal in the world. He folded his hands tightly behind his back to resist the temptation to take it down, to feel the weight of it, just to handle it.

The fire began to crackle in the stove. Brad got down, closed the damper, then shrugged into his parka. He turned the damp down and tiptoed outside.

With the first breath he choked and gasped, as freezing air struck his lungs.

Mickie heard him, and his wolflike head popped out of the

34

doghouse. The next instant he lunged the length of the chain. He looked like a big arctic wolf with his quick gliding steps, his big head down, golden almond eyes slightly narrowed as he watched Brad. Every movement gave the impression that beneath his thick grayish-white coat lightning-swift muscles were ready to spring.

Brad ran to him, gripped his muzzle, and whispered: "Quiet! No barking! You'll wake up everybody. No barking. You hear?"

Mickie whined, put a paw on Brad's arm, and searched his face while the boy unfastened the collar. Then they went plowing through the hip-deep snow toward the hill back of the cabin. It was slow, hard going for Mickie. He sank to his chest. He tried jumping, but sank deeper with each landing. Finally he hunched his shoulders and drove straight ahead, powerful legs bulldozing a chest-deep trail. It took a good twenty minutes to make the short distance to the summit of the gentle rise.

There Brad fell on Mickie, and for the next few minutes boy and dog were all wrapped up in a tumbling, threshing bundle of flying snow and snarling, barking, shouting noise. A stranger would have sworn that a huge wolf, uttering bloodcurdling snarls, was attacking a human and tearing him to shreds.

When they finally stopped, both were out of breath. Mickie lay flat in the snow, head on his forepaws, sharp ears pricked forward and his tongue hanging out. Brad sat on a stump beside him, fingers twisted in the dog's thick fur, and looked down the long sweep of unbroken snow toward the cabin. From where he sat he had the odd sensation that the

35

snow rolled down the slope like a deep carpet, covering rocks, brush, and all imperfections. Even as he looked, a pencil of light shot into the night sky, lightening it and bringing the scene below into dawn-gray relief. The skeleton frame of the little dock was clearly visible, as was the *Annie B,* white against the blue of the sea.

The cabin had been built several hundred feet from the sea. A short distance to the left, Brad made out the hump of a cutbank. In the bank, he guessed, was the freeze room his father had talked about.

Annie and Captain Ed had tunneled into the bank and hacked out a small room in the permafrost, added a door to keep out the summer heat and wild animals, and they had a year-round refrigerator. In it Annie kept the jams and jellies she made from gallons of wild berries she gathered during the summer. In the fall, while the men cut the winter's wood and made the cabin and the *Annie B* snug against the coming winter, she filled the room with game. She'd kill a bear, several deer, a moose, and whatever other small game animals and birds were available. "I watched her skin out a moose once," his father had said. "She was faster than any man I know. With meat a dollar a pound just to fly it in, what she kills makes quite a saving."

The cold began to creep in, but Brad was held by the sheer magic of the scene. Over the absolute silence of the near dawn a million stars looked down. These were not the peaceful, far-off stars of a summer sky. These flashed and sparkled as if fanned to life by a giant wind. The Big Dipper hung suspended directly over the cabin. A thin rope of smoke lifted lazily through the still air toward its bottom.

36

Brad turned and looked behind him. They were at the entrance to a valley that wound away toward a line of snow-blanketed peaks that marched inland until their numbers disappeared in the distance. The first light had come from behind those peaks. Now it grew and spread.

He looked back down the slope. A light had blossomed in one of the ports of the *Annie B.* George, who slept aboard, was getting up. A minute later a square of light spilled from the cabin.

He had better be getting back. Breakfast was not far off.

They made good time returning. Mickie led, and now that he'd had his morning romp, the dog was satisfied to set a sedate pace. They were still minutes away when Brad realized the night was all but spent. He stopped to watch the sunrise.

The sky was fading to pale blue. That turned to pink and spilled down the bowl of the sky, gradually changing to gold. Rays of the rising sun stretched across the earth. Then, suddenly, the day burst from behind the mountains in a silent explosion of light, and the world was bathed in dazzling colors. There were the deep blue of the distant sea, the green of spruce and hemlock, bent almost double with their weight of snow. Countless icy diamonds hung from every branch and twig, catching and holding the cold rays of the sun in a host of dancing rainbows.

Finally they went on to the cabin, where Brad put the collar on the reluctant Mickie. He took off his parka and shook snow from it. With a stick he carefully scraped the snow off his moccasins.

When he stepped into the warm kitchen, Captain Ed and

George were at the table drinking their morning coffee. Captain Ed's black curls glistened with water, and George's thin blond hair was plastered flat to his big skull.

Captain Ed gave Brad a grin and said: "You'd better hurry. Annie's pancakes don't wait for anybody."

George pulled out the chair beside him and said, "There's nothing like a jaunt before breakfast to sharpen the appetite. Eh, Champ?"

From the stove Annie gave Brad a flush-faced grin and said: "Saw you watchin' the sunrise. Pretty, wasn't it?"

Brad nodded. "We don't get that kind at home. There it comes out of the sea and just gradually gets light."

"I know," Annie said, "it's those big mountains inland." And as Brad sat down beside George, she added: "I got up to a nice warm kitchen. You have anything to do with that?"

Brad grinned. "Gram liked it warm when she got up in winter."

"Me, too," Annie said. "But I don't get it too often." She looked at Captain Ed. "It wouldn't take much of this to spoil me through and through."

Breakfast consisted of fluffy sour-dough pancakes, bacon, and fried potatoes. There were coffee for the men and Annie, and chocolate made of canned milk and water for Brad.

During breakfast Annie asked, "What're you fellows doing today?"

"The storm's past," Captain Ed said. "You can have that cruise."

"Can't right now." Annie speared a pancake and buttered it. "I haven't run the trap line since the storm began. Brad and I are gonna run it. Okay with you?" she asked Brad.

38

"I'd like that."

"Fine! Anyway," she went on, "there's no rush about this cruise. We've got all winter."

"Then let's fix that water pump and put the turntable on the stern," George suggested to Captain Ed. "That turntable's going to be a problem. It looks like it hasn't been used for a couple of years."

"Probably hasn't," Captain Ed agreed. "I noticed the seine is pretty old, too. And we may find other things. The *Annie B* hasn't been used for a couple of years either. Remember?"

As the men left after breakfast, George winked at Brad and said: "Take good care of Annie, Champ. She's getting awful weak of late."

Annie dismissed George with a wave. "Back to your bolts and nuts. We'll take care of the real work."

She quickly stacked the dishes in the sink. "Sun's climbin'. We've got to get moving. We'll do the dishes when we get back." She went to the gunrack and saw the pulled-up chair Brad had forgotten to remove.

"I just looked at them," he explained.

"You got a gun?"

He shook his head. "Dad let me shoot his a couple of times."

"You've run a trap line, though. Lots of kids up here run their own trap line."

"I don't know anything about a trap line."

"You can make good pin money running your own line and get a lot of experience."

"There's no animals on Glacier Island to trap. It's real small and all grass and rocks."

Annie shook her head. "No gun, no trap line, and living your whole life on that rocky little island. You haven't got around much or seen much, have you?"

"Mom was afraid I'd get lost or freeze to death or maybe shoot myself or—or something. She was from Seattle. She was always afraid."

"Then we'll start your education now," Annie stepped up on the chair seat. "This top gun is the big rifle, as fine a gun as was ever made. It'll knock down anything in the world. We take it out only when we're after a moose or a brownie or something big."

"Are we taking it today?" Brad asked hopefully.

"Nothing to take it for. This next is a light rifle for smaller game. This is a twelve-gauge shotgun. This last is a twenty-gauge, a small shotgun for ptarmigans"—she pronouned it *tommygan*—"ducks, squirrels, and the like." She lifted down the light rifle and the twenty-gauge. She handed the shotgun to Brad. "You might as well start learning to handle a gun. Shells are in that table drawer. Fill your pockets. Let's get started. We won't have too much daylight."

On the back porch she handed Brad a small woodsman's ax. "Stuff this in your belt. It's the most valuable thing you can carry outside of a gun. And here's a pair of snowshoes. You've been on snowshoes? Good." She slipped an empty tin can in her packsack, ran her arms through the straps, and was ready to go.

Mickie set up a chain-rattling howl to go along. He stood on his hind legs and pawed the air, he was so anxious.

"Can we take him?" Brad asked.

"No," Annie said shortly. "He'll scare the game."

40

Brad squatted in the snow, held Mickie's big head between his hands, and talked to him, trying to quiet him down. He scratched at the base of Mickie's sharp ears and put his cheek against Mickie's warm, furry face. "You can't come," he explained. "I don't like to leave you either. I'd like to take you. You know that. It'd be fun having you hunt with us. But Annie says 'no' and that's it. It's not as if I was leaving you for good. I'll be back in a few hours. So you just be patient and wait."

He patted Mickie's head again, then hurried to catch up with Annie. He glanced back once, and Mickie was sitting in the snow looking forlornly after them.

Brad kept three or four paces behind Annie. He was glad he'd had experience on snowshoes or he wouldn't be going on the trap line run. He held the little twenty-gauge in both hands, balanced across his body so the muzzle pointed away from Annie but so he could swing it around quickly. It was the first time he'd ever carried a gun, and it gave him a wonderful feeling. He hoped something would pop up so he could throw down on it and begin shooting.

They passed the spot where he and Mickie had romped, and entered the valley beyond. It was a broad valley that spread out wide and flat and flowed back into the maze of snow-covered peaks and was lost. The floor was dotted with brush patches, the brush bent double beneath its weight of snow. A line of scrub trees wandered up the center of the valley. Brad knew they marked the banks of a small stream that lay frozen solid beneath the snow. On the right, mountains marched along the rim of the valley. A brush-choked ravine slashed into them, cutting a rule-straight gouge that seemed to run for miles. The opposite side of the valley was bordered by bread-loaf hills that lifted to the flat tundra beyond.

Annie said: "The trap line starts up ahead. It's a two-pronged line. The long line goes straight up the valley. The short one branches off and goes up that deep brushy ravine on the right. We'll run the long one today, the short one tomorrow." She dug the empty can from her pocket, "This's a good place to practice a little. Let's see you hit this can. Hold the butt tight against your shoulder and shoot about six inches ahead. Ready?"

Suddenly Brad was nervous. "It's only a can," he told himself. But he had never fired a shotgun and he had never shot at a moving target.

Annie tossed the can. Brad jerked the gun up, searching frantically. He glimpsed the can tumbling toward the earth, and fired. He shot three feet over it.

Annie said: "Leave the empty in the barrel. Cock the gun and snap the hammer. Take your time. If you don't get on it, don't pull the trigger."

It was the third toss before he snapped the hammer just as the can plopped into the snow.

Annie kept tossing the can, her gravelly voice pouring advice and encouragement at him: "Relax. Take your time. Keep your eye on the can. The gun'll follow. That's better."

He began catching the can at the top of the arc, where it hesitated before starting down.

"Okay," Annie said. "Try another shot."

He caught the can at the top of its arc and drove it a foot higher.

"That's fine." Annie smiled. "Now all you need is plenty of practice. Long as you're here, you consider that little twenty-gauge yours."

"Gee!" Brad ran a hand lovingly down the cold, smooth barrel and along the shining stock. "I can use it any time? I can take it out alone?"

"Not alone yet," Annie said. "You've got a lot to learn. Well, let's go."

At the first stop they took a snow-white weasel. The next two held muskrats, and Annie was feeling good. "Gonna be a nice payday," she remarked as she stuffed them into the packsack.

The fourth trap was sprung. The snow was tramped down, and there were bits of fur lying about. A line of tracks plowed away up the valley.

Annie bent and examined the trap, the tracks, and the surrounding cut-up snow. She moved the torn fur about with a mittened hand. Then for a long moment she just bent there. When she looked up, all her cheerfulness had slipped away. There was near tragedy in her voice, "Oh, Lord!" she said. "We've got a wolverine on the line."

Brad had read about wolverines and he'd heard stories from trappers and his father. The woleverine is the most vicious animal in all the North. His average weight is no more than thirty-five pounds. But he is feared and hated by every living creature and trapper in the country. He is a bloodthirsty killer who slaughters for the sheer pleasure of killing. Not even a grown bear, timber wolf, or mountain lion will challenge him. He is an evil-tempered bundle of raw courage who will attack a man or an animal twenty times

43

his size, and fight it to the death. He had ruined countless trap lines and driven experienced trappers out of the country with his depredations. The native Indians and Eskimos call him "carcajou" or "Indian devil." But his fur is highly prized.

"What'll we do?" Brad asked.

"We've got to try to find him and kill him. If we can't, we might as well pull up the traps and go home," Annie said bitterly. "We're through for the year. He'll haunt this trap line all winter, and tear up every fur we catch. I had one on the line once before. I never did catch him, and he finally forced me to quit."

For three hours they slogged up the widening valley, visiting set after set. Always it was the same. The wolverine had got there first. Several times he had dragged the trap away and buried it deep in the snow—a favorite wolverine trick. They followed the tracks, found the traps, and reset them. At each ruined set, Annie's spirits sank lower. "We've got to get him," she kept mumbling. "We just got to!"

Near the end of the line they found another trap gone, and the wolverine's tracks, dragging the trap, led down into a small ravine.

"I'll set another'n," Annie said. "You follow and dig that one out."

Over the lip of the ravine and out of sight of Annie, Brad clicked off the safety and went sneaking along. "Might see that Indian devil any second. Better be ready. Hold the gun tight to the shoulder and don't jerk the trigger. Squeeze it." He carried the gun pointed forward and down, so he could swing it up fast, and shoot.

The trail led straight into a patch of willows, and in a

small cleared spot near the center it disappeared into the snow. The end of the chain lay in plain sight. He bent to pick it up. At that moment the snow exploded before his eyes, and through it charged the ugly black face of the wolverine, teeth bared, uttering coarse, guttural snarls.

Brad jerked the gun up and pulled the trigger in the animal's face all in one motion. Nothing happened. The wolverine's teeth struck the barrel with a sharp snap. Instinctively Brad threw the animal off, and in so doing lost the shotgun. The wolverine landed a few feet away and charged back to attack, snarling horribly. His short, chunky body and stubby legs are not made for speed and quickness. Brad saw that he was further hampered by the trap that was clamped tight to one front leg.

Brad jumped backward, trying to avoid the charge, looking frantically for some weapon. He remembered the ax and jerked it from his belt. His feet tangled in the snowshoes and he went over backward. The wolverine landed on top of him and clamped its teeth into the first thing he reached, Brad's foot. Brad struck in blind panic at the broad, evil head. He struck again and again. Then he realized there was no further need. The animal lay three feet away. One of those blows had landed squarely between the small, beady eyes. The wolverine was dead.

Brad scrambled up. He was sobbing for breath and he could not stop shaking. He looked at his moccasin. There were two neat holes in the top, but the teeth had not reached his flesh. That had been close, terribly close! He looked at the dead wolverine. Suddenly he was sick, and leaned against a willow clump, waiting for the nausea to pass.

45

He was still there when Annie rushed into the clearing crying, "Brad! Brad!"

She saw him, the ax still in his hand, the dead wolverine. She dropped her rifle and grabbed his arms, "You all right?" she cried anxiously. "You all right?" He was amazed at the strength in her small hands.

"I'm fine," he said. "The—the gun wouldn't shoot."

Annie dug the shotgun out of the snow and inspected it, while Brad explained what had happened. "It's froze up," she said. "But the safety's off. You tried. You did the right thing and you must have done it awful fast. I forgot to tell you that in cold weather you've got to take off your mitt and put your bare hand over the hammer every so often to keep it from freezing. But you used your head. You hand-fought him and you killed him with a belt ax. That was a mighty brave thing to do. No man could have done better."

"I was scared," Brad confessed. "The way he came at me . . . I guess I yelled."

"Who wouldn't?" Annie said promptly. "I've known grown men to run away. And they weren't ashamed afterward, either. What I don't understand"—she nudged the dead wolverine with her toe—"is how he got caught in a trap. They're too smart for that."

"This one wasn't."

"Maybe he got careless or something," she mused. "We'll never know. But you saved the trap line. That's the important thing." She smiled suddenly, her black mood gone. "If you feel up to it, we'd better hit the trail again. It's going to be dark when we get home, and we've got three more traps to

46

go. We can skin this fellow out here and not have to pack all that weight back."

Brad didn't want to return with just the hide. This was the first thing he had ever killed. It had been a very personal triumph in which he'd risked injury, and won. But he couldn't say so. He said: "He's not very heavy. I could carry him, easy."

"It's a long five miles," Annie began, "and in this snow every pound . . ." She glanced up into the boy's face, then looked down at the wolverine. "You're right," she agreed. "George and Ed'll never believe our story if we don't take him back like he is. But let's carry him up and leave him on the trail while we finish running the line."

It didn't take long to cover the remaining three traps, and they caught another mink and a muskrat. At the last trap Annie scraped snow from a log and they sat side by side, guns leaning against the log, while she dug a pair of sandwiches and a Thermos bottle of tea from a huge pocket.

To Brad, they were in a magic world of utter silence, surrounded by a host of towering snow-covered mountains. The sun was bright, but frost crystals glistened in the frigid air. The tea was warm, and after all those miles and his fight with the wolverine, the sandwich was very good. Brad thought of something, and asked: "You said the trap line was important. Why, when you've got the *Annie B* now?"

"Because of all the money we owe Karlson. This trap line is small as trap lines go, but I've been very careful over the years and never taken more fur than we absolutely needed. So the valley is rich, and we can catch a couple thousand

47

dollars' worth with any luck. Suppose next summer the salmon run isn't big or we have some trouble like hitting a rock or tearing up a seine. A lot of things could lay up the *Annie B* for a few days, when every day means big money during the short seining season. This trap-line money might make the difference that would pay off Karlson, if we happened to be a little short. So, you see, killing the wolverine not only saved the trap line, but maybe helped save the *Annie B,* too."

"I'm sure glad I got him," Brad said.

"Me too." Annie slid off the log. "Well, let's go."

On the return trip Brad carried the wolverine and his gun. Annie carried the five animals they'd taken and her rifle. When they finally came out of the mouth of the valley above the cabin, night had folded over the earth. The sky was alive with stars, and a fat moon was riding high above the nest of jagged peaks. It was almost as bright as day, but with an eerie soft light that cast weird shadows across the snow and made lacework patterns of a forest of bare limbs and trees. He could see the bulk of the cabin, the warm, welcoming light of the window and the smoke roping lazily into the still air.

He was dead tired, and starved. The wolverine weighed like lead. But he didn't feel like the same boy who'd left with Annie a few hours ago. That boy had never fired a shotgun, run a trap line, or even seen a wolverine. The change, he felt, was somewhere inside him, and it was a thing he could not explain but could only feel in a vague sort of way.

Mickie heard them and dived to the end of his chain. He set the night ringing with his welcome.

The kitchen door burst open, flooding light across the porch

48

and onto the snow. Captain Ed's voice called: "You're late. We were about to start out looking for you. What took so long?"

Brad dumped the wolverine in the snow in the doorway's light, and Captain Ed and George stared at it.

"That's what took so long," Annie explained proudly. "He like to ruined the trap line and put us out of business. He would have, too, but for Brad. He fought him hand to hand and killed him with his belt ax."

"What?" Captain Ed asked incredulously.

"Look for yourself."

Both men bent and examined the wolverine.

"Why didn't you skin him out instead of lugging in all this weight?" Captain Ed asked.

"This's Brad's wolverine."

Captain Ed nodded. "I guess we'd have figured you were feeding us a big windy if you hadn't. I'm looking at him, and I still can't hardly believe it. A fifteen-year-old boy!" He shook his black head in wonderment.

Mickie kept jumping at the chain, and whining. Brad went over and turned him loose, and Mickie licked his face and pawed at him. Brad patted the thick fur between his ears and said: "I'm glad to see you, too. I wish you'd been along today. You sure could have helped me."

Mickie went over and sniffed at the dead wolverine and growled deep in his throat.

George squatted and turned the wolverine over again and again. "Mick," he said, "you're a good fighter, I'm sure. But this baby would have chewed you up like mincemeat." He examined the head where the ax blade had landed, and said

49

in a wondering voice: "I'm a son of a gun. First day on a trap line and he bags a wolverine. And not with a gun. By hand." He tipped his broad, scar-furrowed face up and studied Brad, rubbing the thick ear thoughtfully between thumb and forefinger as he visualized the short, fierce battle between the slender boy and the vicious animal. In the outpouring light from the doorway the ragged, lumpy brows and deep scars stood out sharply, giving him a tough and ugly look. He said in the soberest voice Brad had ever heard: "Champ, you're quite a boy! Yes siree, Bob. You're quite a boy!"

Somehow those words coming from a man like Big George just fit this new feeling inside him.

three

Brad hadn't dreamed wintertime could be so busy. It had not been with his parents on Glacier Island. Every day George and Captain Ed worked the short daylight hours aboard the boat while Brad and Annie ran the trap line.

They would start when the first gray streaks peeped from behind the cluster of white peaks, and by traveling fast they returned as the brittle sun fell into the frigid sea far to the southwest. With the wolverine gone the catch was again good, and Annie was happy.

The second day Brad had turned Mickie loose. The moment they started out he had followed, tearing gleefully through the snow and leaping about them, barking happily. Annie said harshly, "Make him stay home or tie him up again."

Brad had taken Mickie back, and once again he squatted in the snow, held the dog's big head in his hands, and said: "You can't come. You have to stay here. It's not me. It's

Annie who doesn't want you. When are you going to learn she doesn't like you?" Mickie looked at Brad with big golden almond eyes, and did not understand. His lips were pulled back in a grin, and his plumed tail waved happily. As far as he was concerned he was going.

"You can't come." Brad patted the thick fur between Mickie's sharp ears. "If you want company till I get back, go down to the boat with George and Captain Ed. They'll be glad to have you. But you stay. Understand? Stay."

Mickie understood the word "stay." He lost his grin and his tail drooped dejectedly. "It's not that bad," Brad said. "I'll be back in a few hours, and we can still have our wrestling match every morning." So each morning as they left, Mickie sat dutifully on his tail in the snow and sorrowfully watched them fade into the brittle dawn.

Captain Ed said Mickie hung around the cabin part of the time, then took off hunting on his own. Finally he began going to the *Annie B* with the men. But each night he would be sitting before the cabin, waiting for Brad and Annie, his wolflike head pointed up the slope toward the mouth of the valley, eyes searching for a sight of them. The moment they came into view, he would come lunging through the snow to meet them, setting the twilight ringing with his welcome.

Mickie liked Annie even though she never seemed to notice him. She could not step out the door for a piece of stovewood or to go to the freeze room but what Mickie was there to dog her steps, anxious to be noticed, and waiting patiently for the friendly word she never spoke. Captain Ed asked once, "How can you ignore him when he likes you so much?"

Annie's thin lips pulled into a straight line, but she did not answer.

Annie's ignoring Mickie and refusing to let him accompany them on the trap line were the only disturbing things to Brad. These were almost completely lost in a host of pleasant happenings.

A new and fascinating world was opening for the boy as Annie continued what she called his "education." Now he looked forward to each day as a new and exciting adventure. The first time he shot a ptarmigan on the wing, Annie praised him lavishly and sang those praises to Captain Ed and George that night. "That tommygan shot outa the brush going lickety-split, and Brad ups and lets him have it as cool as you please. He just exploded in a bunch of feathers."

"So we've got a Deadeye Dick in the house," and Captain Ed grinned.

George ruffled Brad's straight hair with a big hand and said: "First you kill the wolverine. Now you're picking off tommygans on the wing. Keep this up and you'll run Annie right outa business, Champ."

"He will for a fact," Annie agreed proudly.

The next day, from a small hill, they watched a pair of wolves run down a snowshoe rabbit. The rabbit, with his heavily furred feet, skipped lightly over the snow, while the heavy wolves sank to their chests. The rabbit easily left them behind. But he made a rabbit's typical mistake and ran in a great circle. The wolves stationed themselves and took turns running him until he was exhausted.

53

Annie let Brad try the light rifle on the wolves, but the distance was too great. They faded into the brush carrying the dead rabbit.

The next morning when Brad took down the guns he asked: "Want me to take the big rifle? Might see those wolves again. I'd sure like to take the big one once."

"Those wolves were just traveling through," Annie said. "And the big rifle's too much gun for you. You stick to the twenty-gauge."

The part of each day Brad enjoyed most was the half hour or so they sat side by side on a log at the end of the trap line eating their sandwiches and drinking the Thermos bottle of chocolate or tea, and talked. The days were clear and the white mountains leaned over them from all directions and the silence was as deep as time. The snow muffled all sound, and it seemed as if they were the only living persons in a white, dead world. It was during one of these talks that he asked, "Where did you get the name 'Stampede Annie'?"

Annie brushed crumbs from her lap, and smiled. "I was about seven or eight, I guess. Mother followed the stampedes in those days and fed the miners. My father'd been killed in a cave-in. Mother would set up a tent and hang out a sign, 'Pancakes, Bacon, and Beans.' Those hungry miners flocked in to eat. This day, I'd heard some miners talking about a new strike. Ours was about to peter out, so I rushed in to tell Mother the news. A couple of miners in there kidded me about going on another stampede. An hour later it was all over camp, and along with everyone else, Mother and I struck our tent, packed the flour, beans, and bacon, and headed for the new one. When we got there the same two fellows came in, and one said, 'Darned if here ain't Stampede Annie again.' The name stuck. When Ed and I were married twenty-five years ago and moved out here, the name 'Stampede Annie' followed."

"You've lived here that long?"

"Moved out on our honeymoon, lived in a tent all summer, and built the cabin with our own hands," Annie said proudly. "For years we had a dog team, and I'd mush the sixty miles into Orca City every winter for our staple groceries, while Ed cut the winter's wood and did other things."

"You can go to Orca City by land from here?"

"Sure. Go up this valley to where that line of mountains curves off to the left, and follow them. They'll lead you right into Orca City's main street. It's easy traveling in winter with everything frozen over and four or five feet of snow. But in summer it's rockslides, marshes swarming with mosquitoes, brush so thick you have to fight your way through, brown-bear meadows full of the critters, and about a hundred ice-cold streams to cross. Even a hairy old prospector would think twice before tackling that hike in summer. A bush pilot hiked out once when his plane motor stalled. He traveled only about thirty miles, but he was a sorry sight."

"When did you stop going in by dog team?"

"When we got our first boat. She was transportation as well as a seiner. She was a leaky old tub, but in seven years we saved enough so that by borrowing from old Karlson we got the *Annie B.*"

"You kept the dogs?"

"Until they died. I couldn't sell 'em." She kicked her small

55

feet in the snow and said thoughtfully, "I watched 'em die, one by one, and then buried 'em."

"I don't think I could do that," Brad said, and knew more about Annie than he'd been told.

"Wasn't easy." Annie slid off the log and began stomping her feet to restore circulation, "Finish your chocolate," she said gruffly. "We'd better start back."

And there was that memorable night when they were returning later than usual, laden down with a good catch. Dusk had caught them a long mile from the cabin. It was a strange dusk with a rainbow haze belting the horizon. It had widened and deepened, seeping upward into the black dome of the sky, warming and lightening it. It patterned the shadows of trees, rocks, and brush to gigantic lengths across the powdery snow.

Annie caught Brad's arm and said in a hushed voice, "Wait, son! Wait up!" Her small, intent face, framed in the parka hood, was turned up to the heavens, her eyes big with childlike wonder. In that brief moment Brad glimpsed something of the little girl Annie once had been. "Listen," she said. "Listen!" Complete silence closed over the valley, as if the very pulse of the world had stopped. Brad found himself holding his breath, waiting. Then in that deathlike stillness the sky began to move.

Giant bars of light shot across the heavens. Ghostlike arms stabbed and darted, appeared and disappeared, then reappeared to writhe in serpentine-like agony as they lit earth and sky with a weird flame. A giant curtain stained deep green and red shimmered across the sky, blotting out the upper dark and making eerie shadows across the tinted snow. The

56

air was filled with sound that beat at Brad's ears with circling hammers. Then it was gone, and the earth lay in utter darkness. Annie's voice said in soft wonderment: "I've seen the northern lights a thousand times, I guess. They always give me goose bumps and make me feel about as big as an ant."

They were still standing there, held in the magic of the night, when the silence was shattered by a prolonged series of high savage cries, bloodcurdling and fearsome. They echoed and reechoed against the mountains and fled down the valley, filling every nook and cranny: the hunting cry of a wolf pack far back among the forbidding peaks. The sound swelled like the wild notes of an organ, then faded away into silence.

From down at the cabin came an answering sound. Like a breath of wind it began, and rose to a high, clear note of sadness and longing. Then it slowly died away, until Brad was not sure just when it ceased. It rose again and again, each time fading away into complete silence before starting up. The part of Mickie that was wolf had come to life this night, and was pouring its heart out calling to its kind.

Captain Ed and George finished repairing the water pump and got the turntable on the stern. The turntable had proved almost too much for two men to handle. But it was finished at last. That night Captain Ed said to Annie: "We've got everything shipshape for now. We won't work on the seine until spring when we can stretch it out on the ground. We're ready for that cruise you wanted."

Annie glanced at Brad. "I guess we can take the day off tomorrow. Can't we?"

"I—I guess so," Brad mumbled. It came as a shock that he'd been here longer than he realized. But each day had been so full the time just slipped away. He sat there for a little, and the men's talk flowed around him as they planned tomorrow's trip. Then he got up, slipped into his parka, and went outside.

The moment the door opened, Mickie's head popped out of the doghouse. Brad got into his snowshoes and, with Mickie leaping happily about him, went up the valley to the high spot where they had romped that first morning. He had to get out of the cabin so he could be alone and think. He sat on a stump, and Mickie reared against his knees and looked up in his face, tongue hanging out in a grin, sharp ears pricked forward expectantly. "No," Brad said. "I don't feel like playing."

He patted Mickie's head and looked down the slope. There were plenty of stars out but only a quarter moon. Even so he made out the cabin, the boat, and the rough line of the sea. A ball of light blossomed aboard the *Annie B.* George must be turning in early or he and Captain Ed had returned to do something.

He looked long at the cabin's dark shape with its lighted window. There were laughter and happiness and the warm feeling of family closeness and safety there. He knew then why he'd been so shaken at Captain Ed's and Annie's words. He wanted to stay. He wanted to become a part of this family just as Big George was. But tomorrow he had to go home, to

The part of Mickie that was wolf had come to life this night, and was pouring its heart out calling to its kind.

being alone with no one to talk with and nothing to do or look forward to, except circling each hopeless day on the calendar.

Mickie stretched upward and licked his face. Brad put his arms around his neck and pressed his cheek against Mickie's forehead. "I'm sure glad I've got you," he said. "I don't know what I'd do alone." Mickie looked at him as if he understood, and Brad ran on, the anguish growing within him: "Annie doesn't like you anyway. For all she cares, you might as well not be here. The way she acts, you're just a nuisance." But that was a small annoyance, not an argument for anything. Whether Annie liked him or not, Mickie was doing fine and was no trouble.

The important thing was, he had told Captain Ed he could stay only a few days. No matter how much you'd like to, you couldn't invite yourself to stay forever. "But there's no big rush to get back," he argued with himself. "I don't have to go tomorrow."

But he had been here nearly two weeks. That really wasn't so long. But it was the longest he'd ever been away from home. That was the thing, of course. It was his home and it needed someone in it. You couldn't let your home just sit there and rot. It had been a good home for fifteen years. His parents had built it and he'd been born there. He owed it all the loyalty he had, no matter what it cost him, "We've got to go home," he said to Mickie. "We belong on Glacier Island. Not here. There's no two ways about it. Tomorrow we've just got to go back. Come on."

When he entered the kitchen, Annie was sitting at the

61

table alone, sewing on the broken seam of a moccasin. Her small head was bent while her brown fingers worked swiftly. In the lamplight he could see the faintest gray tinge to her otherwise smooth black hair.

Without looking up she asked, "Did you get it all thought out?" When he said nothing, she added: "I've gone out there many a time when I had a tough one to think through. It always seemed easier with just the night and the stars and the quiet."

"Captain Ed said he'd take me home when he went on a cruise."

"I figured that was probably it." Annie didn't look up from her sewing.

"I only planned to be gone a few days."

"You think something might be wrong at home?"

"I don't know. I've been here almost two weeks."

"Week and a half."

"That's quite awhile," Brad said. "It's been swell here. Only . . ."

Annie laid down the moccasin and looked at him. He had never seen her eyes so blue. "I know." She smiled. "You've got a home."

"Yes."

She picked up the moccasin, turned it over, and laid it down again. "You've made a snap decision," she said finally. "And snap decisions are no good. You sleep on this. Think it over good from all sides. Then see if you still want to go back in the morning."

He took the problem to bed with him and fell asleep thinking about it. It was the first thing in his mind in the morning. He had looked at it from all sides, but it always came back to the same thing. "I'll make out," he told himself. "There's plenty of food and wood. And I've got Mickie. With Mickie I can make it. In three more months it'll be spring." Gram always said the whole world took a new lease on life every spring. All he had to do was hold tough.

His mind made up, he arose and dressed in the cold room. He found the sheet Big George had made into a hamper to carry his clothes, and piled them in the middle of it.

No one was up yet. He went into the kitchen, put fresh wood on the banked fire, and cracked the damper. Then he stood under the gunrack for a time and looked up at the big rifle on top. He visualized its thundering voice and tremendous killing power. He'd like to have tried it just once before he left. The fire began to crackle and he closed the draft. "Last breakfast here," he told himself.

At breakfast Captain Ed and George were occupied with planning the day's trip. Brad waited for a lull in the conversation to ask Captain Ed to take him home. The moment came and passed. They were near the end of the meal and the men were finishing their coffee when Captain Ed said suddenly, "Hey, you're not eating, Brad. Anything wrong?"

"No." Brad met Captain Ed's black eyes. "I was just thinking. . . ."

"Must be pretty deep stuff when a growing boy forgets to eat," George observed.

"Brad and I are figuring where we wanta go today," Annie said. "We haven't decided yet."

"You'd better make it fast." Captain Ed finished his coffee, and rose. "We'll be ready to pull out in half an hour."

After the men had gone, Brad asked, "You didn't tell him?"

"You were going to sleep on it. Remember?"

"I did. Just like you said, and I've got to go back," he said miserably. "I've just got to. I—I'll get my stuff."

Annie followed him into the front room, where he began pulling up the corners of the sheet in preparation to tying them. She didn't offer to help. Finally she said, "I figured when you thought it all over you'd come up with a sensible decision and stay here."

"I tried," Brad said. "But I can't. That's my home. Besides," he added, not knowing what else to say but feeling he needed further reasons, "I make extra work for you."

"An extra cup and plate and a couple of extra pancakes. For that you ran the trap line with me and carried in most of the fur. And you saved the line when you killed the wolverine."

"You'd have killed him. And you carried in the fur other years."

"Maybe I'd have got the wolverine. I didn't before when I had one on the line. I was mighty discouraged this time I can tell you. As for packin' in the fur," she shook her head. "Those miles get longer and those hills higher and the fur gets heavier every year. There's no use kidding myself. I've about reached the end of that trail. Anyway, I was hoping you'd learned enough in the two weeks you spent alone on Glacier Island and in the time you've been here to know you can't go back there to live."

Brad glanced up. Her thin lips were pulled into a straight line and her small hands were folded tightly behind her back

64

in the now familiar gesture that squared her narrow shoulders and lifted her round chin to that stubborn set. She's going to lay down the law again, he thought.

"I wanted you to make your own decision," she said. "Then I figured you'd be happier here. But I was wrong. You're too young to decide anything important. You're still a little kid. So I'm going to do it for you."

He was stung by her blunt words and rough tone. "I lived there alone," he said. "I proved I can. I killed the wolverine. You said yourself no man could have done better. What do you mean, I'm too young?"

"You didn't have to think to kill the wolverine or to live alone on Glacier Island. Those things were forced on you."

"Then how old, how big do I have to be to decide what I'm going to do?"

"Not old in size," Annie said thoughtfully. "Not old in years. Old in grown up."

"What's that?"

"I'm not sure I can explain it. Maybe that's because I don't really know what it is. But it's in here." She tapped her chest. "Something makes you big inside, sort of takes out the boy and puts in the man. I know it when I see it. Maybe killing the wolverine and living alone a couple of weeks would help. But not near enough. You haven't got it yet. I know that. So I'm making this decision for you. Why, I couldn't sleep nights if I let you go back there alone. So you're staying here till spring. We'll go past your place today and make sure everything's locked up tight and we'll bring back all the food and stuff that might spoil, and get the rest of your clothes. From time to time we'll cruise that way and check the house.

65

And you and I'll go right on running the trap line and eating our sandwiches and drinking our chocolate on a stump and watching the northern lights and catching fur. What's wrong with that?"

It was just about perfect, Brad thought. As long as they would be checking his home, he wasn't deserting it. "I think it's swell." He grinned. Then he remembered something, and asked, "You said till spring. What happens then?"

"Maybe nothing. But come spring we have to write your aunt, you know."

For a few days he'd almost forgotten his Aunt Clara. Now the thought of her was like an electric shock. "Why?" he demanded.

"Because," Annie repeated, as inflexible as she'd been that first night, "she's your aunt and it's the right thing to do."

"But I told you she's not interested in me," he said desperately. "I don't mean anything to her. I don't know her and she don't know me. Why can't we just forget her?"

"Because we can't. But if it's like you say, we'll make your staying here a permanent arrangement. That okay?"

"That'd be fine." Happiness gushed through Brad.

"That's the kind of talk I wanted to hear," and Annie grinned.

A shrill whistle sounded from the dock. "They're ready," Annie said excitedly. "Come on. Let's go." She drew back her foot and kicked the hamper with all her strength, scattering Brad's clothes across the floor. "Leave 'em," she laughed. "We've got all winter to pick 'em up." Together they charged through the kitchen and out the door.

Mickie shot out of the doghouse and bounded circles

66

about them, barking excitedly and whipping his tail as they raced down the path to the dock and jumped aboard. Just as the *Annie B* began pulling away from the dock, Mickie sat on his tail, pointed his nose at the sky, and began to howl mournfully.

"Can't he come? Just this once?" Brad begged.

"Why not?" Annie waved her arms expansively. "Come on, Mickie," she shouted, and clapped her hands. "Come on, jump. Jump, Mickie!"

Mickie raced along the dock, barking excitedly.

"Jump!" Brad urged. "You can make it. Jump, Mickie! Jump!"

Mickie gathered his courage, and leaped. He sprawled on the deck at Annie's feet. She patted his head, laughing, her voice deep and gravelly and happy. Brad didn't know whether she was laughing at Mickie's antics or because she was happy at the thought of her first trip in the *Annie B*.

four

Brad and Annie continued their daily routine of running the trap line. The weather settled down to cold, bright days in which the sun burst from behind the cluster of peaks and flooded the earth a few hours with dazzling light.

Now that there were no blizzards in the making, the snow fields became crisscrossed with whole networks of wild-animal tracks. Learning to read them was like learning to read the pages of a book. Annie showed him where a pair of wolf tracks ran beside those of a floundering deer. Coyote and fox tracks followed those of rabbits, their favorite food. She pointed out where a marten had crept up on an unsuspecting ptarmigan. A small scattering of feathers told the end of the story. Here a deer had backed against a cutbank to make a last valiant but futile stand against a hungry wolf. The struggle had been short and brutal.

"That's how it goes," Annie said. "Everything lives off

something else. Even us. I've been trapping these animals ever since we moved here because we needed the extra money. If everything pans out all right this coming fishing season, I'll quit trapping. We won't need the extra money any more. I hope it works out. I don't much like to kill game except for food."

Captain Ed and George took a job freighting with the *Annie B*. It lasted more than a month. It seemed a good opportunity to pick up several thousand dollars. They returned bitterly disappointed. The freight hadn't come up to expectations. They'd been paid by weight, and they'd spent most of their time and money waiting for loads. "What little we made," Captain Ed said disgustedly, "went for fuel and our own keep. Moneywise we didn't break even and we gave the *Annie B* an awful workout. Now we'll have to take down the motor and work it over before fishing season. Brad," he added, "we went past your place. Everything's shipshape."

Mickie continued to follow Annie at every opportunity. Except for the morning when he'd jumped aboard the *Annie B*, she didn't speak to him or touch him again. But every morning Mickie watched them leave, and every night he was sitting on his tail, head pointed toward the valley, searching for them. Brad didn't know how the big wolflike dog knew when they'd return. But he never missed.

Brad became a good shot with the little twenty-gauge. Annie said one night, "When he pulls down on a running rabbit or a flying tommygan, he's just the squeeze of the trigger away from the pot."

The next morning as Brad stood on the chair to take down

the guns in preparation for starting out, he said: "Maybe I should take the big rifle. I might get a shot at that wolf we saw hanging out near the pothole trap."

Annie shook her head. "You stick with the twenty-gauge. That's your size."

"You said I was good with the twenty-gauge. How'll I ever learn to handle the big rifle if I don't start?"

"There's plenty of time for the big one," Annie said. "You're still a boy. Bring the twenty-gauge."

So the big rifle remained on the rack, shining and inviting.

Annie hadn't mentioned writing to Aunt Clara. So for days at a time it remained only a vague worry that nibbled at the back of Brad's mind.

Then they missed a day running the trap line because Annie wanted to do some baking. Brad and Mickie had gone down to the *Annie B.* He was standing on the turntable in the stern with Mickie beside him looking across the infinite blue sea and listening to the steady sound of hammering coming from below, when the white nose of a boat poked into view around a point a mile away. It was the mail boat, the *Vixen,* on her twice-a-month trip around the Sound.

Brad watched the *Vixen* creep in, then swing broadside and stop an arm's length from the stern of the *Annie B.* Captain Bob Masters stepped from the wheelhouse with a handful of letters. He held them out to Brad and said: "Found your place locked up and figured you might be here. Is your grandmother here, too?"

"She died. I'm staying here now."

"That's tough. I'm sorry. There's a letter here for your grandmother."

70

Brad waited until the *Vixen* was out of sight, then searched through the mail and found the letter. He recognized his aunt's handwriting. A shock that felt like a punch in the stomach rolled through him. He could guess the contents and he knew he had to open it. He listened to the work sounds coming from the engine room. Annie was baking up at the cabin. He would not be interrupted. He tore the letter open and read it.

Aunt Clara was annoyed that Gram hadn't answered her last letter. Spring was coming and summer would soon be here. It was time they thought of Brad's starting to high school in Seattle. There were decisions to make, things that must be done beforehand. Clothes must be bought for Brad. She'd have to move to a larger apartment closer to the school she'd chosen. Brad should get acquainted ahead of time with some of the young people he'd be going to school with. Both she and Brad needed to get well settled before fall classes began.

There was more, but Brad didn't read it all. Aunt Clara was crusading again, and with real fire in her eyes. Annie and Captain Ed must never see this letter. He returned the letter to the envelope, found a small bolt on deck, put it into the envelope, and folded the torn end tightly closed. He dropped the letter overboard and watched it sink out of sight. The remainder of the mail he carried up to Annie.

After that, he held his breath each time the mail boat came, but there were no further letters from Aunt Clara. He told himself that her crusading fervor had just taken a spurt and then cooled off. In time he almost came to believe it.

So the winter months passed, and to Brad each day held

71

some new adventure or some new and wonderful thing learned about this land where he'd been born. He was amazed at how little he knew about the country or life beyond Glacier Island. Now he was seeing it all through Annie's bright blue eyes and learning to love it as she did. For, as she said, "There's not a foot of this valley and these hills I haven't left my boot prints on."

There came a time when their catch ran heavily to beaver and muskrat. Annie said then: "Season's getting short. Spring isn't far off. Beaver and muskrat are getting more active. They know spring breakup is close."

Almost imperceptibly the daylight hours began to lengthen as the sun worked higher in the sky.

Soon after that, Annie announced one morning: "This'll be our last run. It's time to quit. We'll take up the traps."

It took days to carry in the traps, dry them off, and hang them up to await another season. On the last day, they surveyed the pile of furs, and Annie proclaimed it good. "Not bad," she said in her deep voice. "Not bad at all."

"Did we make what you thought we should?"

"We sure did. And you packed most of that catch in on your back." She studied Brad a moment. "You've changed some: added about ten pounds of trail muscle and growed up a little in here." She tapped her chest with a brown finger.

Brad felt he'd changed, too. The little twenty-gauge felt as if it belonged in his hands. He bet the big rifle would, too. He was sure he could run the line alone next year.

He saw the miracle of spring come to the North as he had never seen it on Glacier Island. Slowly the daylight hours burned the snow off the beach. The valley and the ravine where they'd trapped lost its mantle of white. On the low, rolling hills patches of green and yellow tundra rose through the snow. Snow melted off the bent trees and brush, letting them straighten so gently scarcely one was broken. He mentioned this to Annie, and she said, "Nature takes care of its own—the trees, bushes, the animals, the birds."

And it was so.

The ptarmigans, snowshoe rabbits, weasels, and a host of other animals were changing from white to browns and grays to blend with the new season rushing down upon them. Small animals that had spent the winter beneath the snow came out to dart about in a frantic search for food. The icy ribbon of the stream appeared. The ice turned to slush beneath the sun, then one day began its slow march to the sea. On the valley floor green shoots pushed through the dead brown of last year's grass clumps.

With the trapping season over, Annie did not go out so often, so Brad and Mickie were on their own. It was wonderful having Mickie along, and together they explored the valley. Mickie led the way, tail waving, a happy grin lifting his lips as he investigated every bush, brush patch, rock, and hole.

On small, rocky Glacier Island there had always been only the salty tang of the sea. Here Brad was amazed to learn he could smell the spring. Sitting on the log where he and Annie had eaten their sandwiches during the winter, he was aware of the mustiness of deep canyons and the fresh, biting scent flowing down off the high snowy peaks. The heady fragrance of bare limbs bursting into full leaf was laced with the delicate aroma of millions of small flowers blanketing the sun-warmed earth.

With an arm around the restless Mickie to hold him quiet, Brad listened to the sounds of the earth waking from its winter sleep. There were the soft rustle of small moving bodies in the grass and brush, the furtive scratching of tiny claws, the velvety beat of wings. And there were louder, more insistent sounds. A pair of jays made a racket in the thicket, only to be drowned out by the hoarse cries of a horde of crows. From the top of a dead snag an eagle spread his wings and announced to the world that he was hungry. The trumpet call of a *V* of geese winging their way farther north filtered down from a great height. A flight of ducks fled down the valley and landed in the creek. Their excited gabbling told how glad they were to be back.

Several days later Brad saw his first brown bear close up. He and Mickie were passing a patch of willows when the bear ambled into the open no more than a hundred feet away. They were downwind of him, and Brad stood perfectly still, watching him wander onto the valley floor, sniffing along like a searching pig. He was thin and his winter coat was rough. But great ropes of muscles bunched and played sinuously under his loose-fitting hide.

Mickie charged, bellowing furiously. The bear stopped and kept turning to face the circling dog. Suddenly the bear rushed with a full-throated roar of rage. He was the picture of utter destruction as he bore down on Mickie, great head lowered, teeth bared in a savage snarl. Brad wanted to shout a warning to the dog. He couldn't fight such an animal. But the words piled up in his throat and he just stood there terrified, and watched.

Mickie knew he could not fight the bear, too. He danced away. He had no trouble staying beyond the bear's reach. Brad saw why. The bear was favoring one front paw and was running practically on three legs.

He told Annie about it when he got back. She was baking a blueberry pie, and said: "That was Old Toughy. He's got a bum leg, from a fight or something. It bothers him a lot in the spring. But once he gets it limbered up he can run pretty good. He's meaner than sin. He'll charge anything, including a man. I watch him mighty close in the spring. You were lucky you were downwind of him. You'd better not go any farther than the head of the valley, after this."

"If he's dangerous why don't you shoot him?" Brad asked.

"Mostly he don't bother. He winters 'way back in the hills someplace. In the early spring he comes down to eat grass and skunk cabbage and dig roots on the valley floor. When the salmon run starts, he goes back up in the hills. He's got a special spot that he's staked out up there on the creek where he fishes. So when I'm out picking berries or getting our winter meat he's not around. No sense killing him for the little time he's down here. Did you see any salmon in the creek? The first ones oughta be along soon."

Brad did know about the salmon run and what it meant to the North. He'd heard talk of runs and salmon ever since he could remember.

Everyone in the Sound made his living from the salmon run. It kept Orca City and a dozen other villages along the coast alive. It supported the seven canneries in the Sound.

75

more than a thousand seiners that came north from the States, and the thousands of workmen that migrated with them to work in the canneries and aboard boats. Even the animals and birds owed their existence to the migrating salmon. The brown bears congregated along the spawning streams, where they ate their fill and grew fat. Gulls, foxes, crows, eagles, and hawks vied with the bears for their rightful share. At sea, herds of seals and sea lions charged into salmon schools, into the seiners' nets, and even into the fish traps to gorge themselves. This feverish activity would last a month to six weeks. In that short time all the wildlife would have eaten its fill, the canneries would have put up their packs of thousands of cases, and the fishermen must have made their year's wages.

Soon Brad saw boats going by, far at sea. The seiners from the States were beginning to arrive. One day a cannery tug hove into sight towing a pile driver and raft of pilings. Off some point those pilings would be driven into the sea bottom to form a fish trap that might catch half a million salmon in a season. When George and Captain Ed stretched the nine-hundred-foot seine on the beach and began patching it, Brad knew the time was short.

Two days later, on a hike up the valley, Brad, Annie, and Mickie saw a pair of slim torpedo shapes nosing along the clear, pebbly bottom. "Look!" Annie cried excitedly. "There they are! The first salmon are here! The run's about to start. That's the vanguard." They lay on their stomachs on the bank above and watched for several minutes. Mickie crawled up between them and stared into the water, too. "When the run is really on," Annie said, "this bottom right along here will have a hundred fish, maybe more. I've seen 'em so thick you couldn't see bottom. Just think, those two were born right here four years ago. They've been all around the world, probably. Now they're back, ready to spawn themselves. Then their eggs'll hatch and it'll start all over again."

Mickie turned his head suddenly and touched her cheek delicately with his black nose. Annie rose, brushed off her knees, and said gruffly, "Let's go."

When they told the men that night, Captain Ed said: "We'll finish the seine just in time. Now I'm wondering where I can hire a good pickup man to round out the crew."

"You worry about that every year," Annie said.

"And I'm worrying about it again."

"Does the extra man have to know all about the sea and boats?" Brad asked.

George shook his head. "He's a pair of extra hands. Helps handle the seine, helps brail, takes his turn watching for fish. Things like that."

Brad looked at George and Captain Ed, and then at Annie. "Why can't I go and do that? Dad said he'd take me this year."

"You want to go fishing with us?" Captain Ed asked, surprised.

"I'm big enough. You even said I was."

Captain Ed rubbed his long jaw thoughtfully. "Well," he said finally, "I don't know."

"He's right," George added. "You did say it—in a way."

"I wasn't thinking of him going aboard the *Annie B* then."

77

"He's not going," Annie said.

"You don't need me here this summer, and they do need another man." Brad argued directly with Annie now. "You said yourself I carried in most of the fur. And I never tired out once. And you said I'd grown up some. Remember?"

"But not that much. Fifteen is still fifteen."

"You said it wasn't years old that mattered," Brad reminded her. "And George said all they needed was another pair of hands. Well, I'm another pair of hands." Then he threw his big argument at Annie. "You said we needed the trap line because the couple of thousand dollars it made might help pay off the *Annie B* if there was any trouble. If Captain Ed hires another hand, he'll have to give him a share of the catch. That could be as much as four thousand dollars. That's twice what the trap line made. So it's twice as important for me to go along and help with the seining. You don't have to pay me because—because I'm part of the family— just like George." All three looked at him and said nothing. "You treated me like I was part of the family," he said desperately. "I—I thought . . ." He bogged down, at a loss to continue.

Annie said, "You've been part of this family since the first night you stood in this kitchen."

"That's right," Captain Ed agreed. "So let's hear no more of that."

George rubbed his muffin-thick ear and studied Brad thoughtfully from beneath lumpy brows. "Champ," he said finally, "you're quite a scrapper! No wonder that wolverine didn't have a chance."

"Then I've got to do my share," Brad insisted.

Annie looked at Captain Ed. "Do you think he could pull his weight?"

"Young fellows no bigger or huskier than Brad have been on boats before. I don't see why not."

"I can teach him all he needs to know in no time," George offered.

Annie rubbed her small hard hands together, frowning intently. Finally she looked at Brad. "With Ed and George you couldn't be safer. All right," she agreed, "I guess you've got a summer job. Now there's just one other problem. What about Mickie? What'll you do with your dog?"

"He can stay here with you," Brad said.

"Not a chance!" Annie's voice had turned tough and uncompromising. "I told you to begin with I don't have time to fool with a dog."

"Be reasonable, Annie! What can we do with him?" Captain Ed asked.

"Take him aboard the boat with you. Let him stay there."

"A boat's no place for a dog."

"As much a place as here with me. I've got work to do. I've got to gather, can, and jell and jam about twenty gallons of berries. Later I've got to kill, butcher, and pack in our winter meat. I can't be bothered."

"Can't or won't?" Captain Ed demanded.

"Suit yourself." Annie's small chin came up in that stubborn set.

"I've seen plenty of dogs aboard boats," George said gently. "We can manage."

"I'll take care of him," Brad said. "I'll keep him out of the way."

Captain Ed scowled and dug his fingers through his black hair. "Okay," he agreed finally. "We'll give it a try. We can sure use you. But I don't like it. I don't like it at all." ·

"Can't be helped," Annie stated. Then, as if the subject was closed, she asked, "How soon do you plan to leave?"

"Season opens in five days. If we leave day after tomorrow, that'll give us a day to make the cannery, another to gas up and check where the fish are running, and a couple of days to get on the fishing grounds."

"Then we'll have to get everything on board tomorrow. You get your clothes there," Annie said to Brad. Then she noticed how his wrists stuck out of the cuffs of his shirt. "Ed, when you get to the cannery take Brad in the store and get him a couple of shirts that fit."

The next day Brad got his clothes aboard and stowed them beneath one of the bunks. He took the collar and chain from the doghouse, just in case he might have to tie Mickie to keep him out of the way.

That night, after supper, when the table had been cleared, Annie got out writing paper and ink. "Got to write that letter for you to mail to Brad's aunt," she explained.

"Why?" Brad demanded instantly. "She's two thousand miles away. She's never even seen me."

"She's your aunt, your only relative. We've been all over this a couple of times," Annie said. "I've let it go as long as I can. Now I'm going to write her."

Brad knew it was useless to argue against Annie's iron determination, but he couldn't help himself. "This is my home. Not down there in some city like Seattle. I'm going to be a seiner like Captain Ed, like my father was. So why should I leave here?"

"You think she'll want you to go to the States?" Captain Ed asked.

"I don't know. But suppose she does?"

"If she thought anything of you, she would," Annie said. "But if she's not interested, like you say, you've got nothing to worry about. So let's not borrow trouble."

He was stymied. Annie's last statement had backed him into a corner from which he didn't dare say more without revealing what he knew of his aunt's intentions.

"What are you going to write her?" he asked fearfully.

"Just what happened to your grandmother, that you're living with us, and that we're keeping an eye on the house."

"Will you tell her that I want to stay? That this is my home and always will be?"

Annie considered, nibbling the end of her pen thoughtfully. "No," she said finally. "If she's the kind of woman you say, it won't matter. On the other hand, it could look like we're trying to pick an argument with her over you. That could rile her up. We'd better just state the facts and let it go at that."

Captain Ed nodded. "Let sleeping dogs lie."

George stared at his big feet thrust out before him, rubbed his ear, and said nothing.

"Now everybody be quiet," Annie said, "and let me write this letter."

Brad watched her composing the letter, her thin lips forming each word under her breath. Thinking of what she was writing, and of his aunt getting the letter, made him so nervous he had to go outside.

Mickie joined him, tail waving and looking expectant. Brad was standing there absentmindedly scratching the dog's ears when George came through the door. He looked down at Brad. "Your aunt wants you to come to the States," he announced. "She always has, hasn't she?" When Brad looked up, surprised, he added: "I watched you read the letter the mail boat brought. I saw you drop it overboard."

"I—I didn't see you," Brad stammered.

"I'd just come into the wheelhouse for some tools."

"I didn't know what to do. I don't want to leave here. Thanks for not telling."

"Man has to fight for what he wants, any way he can," George said quietly.

"What'll I do, George?" Brad begged in a panic.

George rubbed his ear thoughtfully. "I've thought a lot about that." He shook his big head. "Nothing you can do, Champ. You'd better face up to the fact that this is one fight you can't win."

"Why, George? Why?"

"Your aunt holds the whip hand, as I see it. You're a minor, and she's your only living relative and she wants you. No fifteen-year-old boy can ever beat an adult in a case like this."

For a long time after George had gone to the boat, Brad sat on a corner of the woodpile on the back porch with an arm around Mickie. He kept thinking of the big man's words. He felt trapped and helpless.

The light finally went out in the kitchen. For a little while he heard the low murmur of Captain Ed's and Annie's voices. Then it was quiet. He guessed he'd better get some sleep, too. He gave Mickie a few final pats and said, "You'd better get a good night's sleep, because tomorrow you're going aboard the boat," and tiptoed into the kitchen.

The finished letter was on the table, propped against the sugar bowl. He picked it up and held it in his hands. The course of his whole life, his plans and dreams and hopes were at stake in that letter. The temptation to tear it up was almost more than he could stand. But it would do no good. Annie would just write another.

He put the letter back, went into the front room, undressed, and crawled into bed. He thought of going aboard the boat tomorrow and taking the place of a man, of doing his share to help pay off the *Annie B*. He thought of Mickie aboard the boat. That wasn't going to be easy. He hoped it worked out and Mickie wouldn't be too much trouble. But those were minor problems. The all-important worry was the letter propped against the sugar bowl in the kitchen.

five

Annie was down at the dock to see them off next morning. She stood, small fists on hips, her voice nagging at them. "You sure you've got everything—boots, sou'westers, slickers? You got all the grub packed? How about salt, sugar, coffee, and chocolate for Brad? You got the chocolate, Ed? Brad, I know you've got your clothes aboard. Now, don't you let Ed forget to buy you a couple of shirts that fit, and get the arms long enough. You hear, Ed? Remember the shirts for Brad."

Captain Ed said finally, "Annie, relax. Everything's under control."

"You got the light rifle? You're apt to need it for seals or sea lions."

"Well, no," Captain Ed confessed.

"I knew you'd forget something," Annie said triumphantly.

84

Mickie ducked about among all the activity, plumed tail snapping, vitally interested in all that was going on.

At last Captain Ed went up to the cabin and returned with the light rifle. "Guess we're ready to go now." He kissed Annie, smiling down at her from his lean height. "Here we go again. Another year, another dollar. How long have we been doing this?"

"Long time," Annie said. "I don't want to remember back. Some of it was mighty tough."

"Different this year," Captain Ed said gently. "Going to be different from now on. We've got the *Annie B* now. There's not a better seiner on the Sound."

"Different other ways, too," Annie said. "We got a boy."

"We sure have!" Captain Ed smiled into Annie's blue eyes. His big hand patted her narrow shoulder gently. "We sure have."

"You remember that, and don't let anything happen to him."

"You think I might forget? You think I might let something happen?"

"Of course not," Annie said promptly. "I'm just warning you, that's all." She raised her voice and shouted at George: "Don't you go loadin' Brad down too much. He ain't half a giant, like you. Remember, he's still just a boy."

George winked at Brad. "What do you mean, 'a boy'? Why, I'll bet he could pull the seine alone if he tried."

"You better be sure he don't try," Annie warned. "I'll nail your hide to the wall if you do."

"Quit worrying." Captain Ed smiled. "We'll do fine.

You'd better take it a little easier. Don't half kill yourself making all that jam and jelly. We can do with a little less."

"No, we can't. There's four of us now. If I made less you'd all throw a Grade A conniption fit. Don't you worry about me. You just take care of the *Annie B* and Brad."

She held Brad's thin shoulders with small hard hands and studied him with shining eyes. "You ran the trap line all winter and killed the wolverine by hand and now you're going to take the place of a man, and seine all summer. Your education is coming along mighty fast."

"I hope I do all right," Brad said. "I want to do my share."

"You'll do fine. Just like you did on the trap line. But eat plenty, hear? Eat till you feel like you're gonna bust. You're a growin' boy. It takes a lotta fuel to grow and work, too. And you be careful," she warned. "Don't take any chances. None at all. That sea's like ice, if you fall in. Even if you can swim, you wouldn't last no time."

"I'll be careful," Brad promised. "You be careful, too, You'll be all alone."

"Don't worry about me. I've been alone for twenty-five summers out here."

The motor of the *Annie B* kicked over. Brad grabbed Mickie, shoved him aboard, and jumped after him. He stood on the turntable in the stern with Mickie beside him as the *Annie B* began to pull away from the dock.

The stretch of water widened, and suddenly Mickie began to bark frantically at Annie. Annie called across the spreading void, "Remember! feed him just once a day."

"I will," Brad answered. He watched Annie grow smaller

and smaller. Finally she turned and went slowly up the trail toward the cabin.

They made Orca City late that afternoon and pulled in to the Orca City Cannery dock and tied to the float. It was the third time Brad had ever been here.

Orca City was a typical Alaskan fishing village of some four hundred permanent residents. It perched on a narrow ledge a few feet above the sea. Its single mud and boardwalk street cut straight through the center of town to the mountains, which stretched away as far as the eye could see. Orca City had a gold-rush history. But the gold had long ago been mined. For fifty years the town had owed its life to the yearly salmon run and the seven canneries along the coast. During the short season the population swelled to as many as several thousand when people poured in to work in the canneries or to go aboard the fleet of seiners that churned north from as far south as California and even Mexican waters to dip into the annual silver harvest.

The mooring basin held only a couple of dozen seiners. "A week ago there must have been close to a thousand here," George observed. "All but these few have already taken off for the fishing grounds."

"Then the fish must be running," Captain Ed said. He held the letter to Brad's aunt in his hand. "I'll go uptown and mail this. You two lock up the boat. I'll meet you at the cannery store in a few minutes."

Brad watched his high shape swing along the float and climb the stairs, the letter still in his hand. He had that sick, empty feeling again, and asked, "George, how long does it take a letter to get to Seattle?"

87

"Couple of days." George dropped a big hand on his shoulder. "Worrying won't help, Champ. I learned a long time ago that the things I worried most about didn't always happen, or when they did, they weren't always as bad as I thought they'd be. Come on, let's go get those shirts."

It was some minutes before they were ready to leave. When they did, Mickie trotted importantly ahead of them and up the stairs, investigating everything with his nose as he went.

The store was one end of the cannery building. It was a long room, packed with a series of shelves that lined the walls. Aisles of portable counters were piled with an assortment of clothes, canned goods, tools, and foods. Here seiners could stock up on all their needs. The bill would be charged against future salmon deliveries.

The store was owned by Karlson, the cannery owner, and was run by Charlie Frost, a bald, lean old fisherman.

Charlie leaned against a counter, faded eyes twinkling. "A couple of shirts for you, George? You need a tent."

"For the boy," George said.

"Didn't know you had a boy." Charlie turned toward the back of the store, and they followed.

Mickie began nosing about among the counters. This was the first store he'd ever been in, and it was filled with a host of curious and fascinating things. Crouched in a round ball on the edge of a counter, and half asleep in a shaft of sunlight, was a black cat. It was the first cat Mickie had ever seen. He thrust an inquisitive black nose close, and sniffed.

The cat opened amber eyes and regarded the dog. He was

88

an old hand at handling the local breeds. He rose leisurely to his full height, settling his rear legs firmly beneath him. The black nose came close for another sniff.

At that moment Brad turned and looked for Mickie. "No! Mickie! No! No!" he yelled. "Get away!"

The cat struck with a full-armed sweep. Sharp claws raked across the dog's tender nose.

Mickie reared back with a startled yelp of pain.

Brad dived for Mickie, and Mickie leaped for the cat. Brad's dive was a foot short, and he fell headlong into a counter, bringing down a shower of clothes. Mickie's snapping jaws missed by a hair as the surprised cat bounced into the air. He hit the floor running, and dug out for the far end of the store with Mickie right at his heels.

Before Brad could get up, cat and dog had dashed between George's legs. The cat, looking for any refuge, raced up Charlie Frost's back to his shoulder. Mickie leaped for the cat, struck Charlie from behind with his solid hundred pounds, and drove the old man headfirst into a tier of shelves loaded with cooking utensils.

When Brad finally gained his feet the cat was squirting up one aisle and down the next, dodging under, around, and over counters in a frantic effort to shake the raging Mickie. But Mickie refused to be shaken. He was out for blood, cat's blood.

Brad raced up and down aisles, screaming at Mickie. George shouted and ran. Charlie Frost yelled at the dog, at the cat, at Brad and George. Pots, pans, canned goods crashed and rolled on the floor. The cat was spitting and yowling. Mickie, ears flattened, jaws wide, showing every tooth in his head, was bawling bloody murder at every jump. The quiet store had been turned into a madhouse.

The cat veered suddenly and headed toward the front of the store with Mickie straining at his tail. Brad tried to head them off but couldn't make it. George almost did. He swung his arms wide as he ran to trap Mickie. His foot hit a rolling can of soup. Both legs shot into the air. He did a complete somersault and landed on his back with a bone-rattling jar. Cat and dog raced squalling and growling the full length of him.

Charlie Frost bawled to no one: "Open th' door! Let 'em out! Let 'em out!"

As though in answer, the front door opened and Captain Ed started in. The cat shot through the opening, along the dock, and ran ten feet up a piling to squat on the top.

Mickie, in mad pursuit, leaped into Captain Ed's surprised arms, and was captured.

Charlie Frost, George, and Brad bore down on Captain Ed, who was holding the struggling Mickie and looking about in amazement. Brad took Mickie, cuffed his ears, and said: "Stop that! Be still. Hear? Be still." He set Mickie on the floor and kept a tight grip on the thick fur of his neck.

"What went on here?" Captain Ed asked.

"We've had quite a ball," George panted.

"A ball is right." Charlie Frost sat down tiredly on the edge of a counter and looked about the store. Counters were overturned and smashed; tiers of shelves had fallen; and the floor was littered with a conglomeration of clothes, tools,

90

utensils, and foods of all kinds. He shook his head in amazement. "That cat an' dog done this in less'n a minute."

"With a little help from us," George added.

Charlie began to chuckle. "That was one surprised cat. I've known for a long time that someday he'd pick the wrong dog. I'll bet it's a long time before he makes another pass at one."

"It wouldn't have happened if he hadn't scratched Mickie," Brad said.

"Maybe not," Charlie agreed. "But that wolf's the fastest thing I've ever seen on four legs."

"He's a Malamute," Brad said.

"Malamute, nothing. He looks like a wolf; moves like one, too. He's greased lightning."

"We'll help you clean up the place and get everything back in place," Captain Ed offered.

Charlie shook his head. "Now that the seiners are all out on the fishin' grounds I've got plenty of time. I'll do it. Besides, I know where everything goes."

"I'm sorry it happened," Captain Ed said.

"It was worth it." Charlie smiled. "I've waited a long time to see that cat tackle the wrong dog. He's been too smart for his own good. You fellows go on. I'll take care of this."

"The shirts for Brad," George said.

Charlie Frost looked around. "We can find 'em. It'll take a little time."

"We'll be back in soon as we seine our first load," Captain Ed said. "Have them ready then."

They were about to leave when the door opened and a

man came in, followed by the biggest dog Brad had ever seen.

Brad knew who the little man was immediately. He'd heard enough from his father, Gram, and Annie to know that this was tightfisted Frank Karlson, the owner of the Orca City Cannery. He was small, with a round little potbelly spilling over his belt and a thin fringe of hair circling a bald head. He had black eyes set close together beneath ragged brows that met over his nose. His mouth was round, thin-lipped, and tight.

He stood braced on stumpy legs, cheeks quivering with anger as he looked around the store. "What happened here? Who did this?" His voice was as high and sharp as a file grating on metal.

"We had kind of a ruckus—" Charlie Frost began.

"Kind of!" Karlson yelled, his round belly shaking. "Th' place's wrecked. You call this kind of a ruckus? What happened? Who did it?"

"Old Black Tom picked on the wrong dog this time," Charlie Frost explained. "The dog come in with the boy and George. Old Tom took a swipe at the dog, and they went round and round. . . ."

Karlson glared at Brad, then shifted his eyes to Mickie. "Call that a dog? That's a wolf. Your wolf wrecked my store, kid."

"The cat opened the ball—" George began.

"Wouldn't been no ball if that—that wolf hadn't been in here," Karlson fairly yelled.

"Maybe not. But that cat needed a lesson and he got it," George said.

92

Captain Ed said quietly to George, "I'll handle this." He turned to Karlson: "No wolf, Frank. A Malamute, a sled dog. I'm sorry this happened. I know it's quite a mess. We'd like to help Charlie clean it up, but he says 'no.' He knows where everything goes, and we don't. I'll pay the damages, of course."

"You just bet you will!" Karlson snapped. "Place's a wreck. Look at it! Just look at it. It'll take a week to get everything sorted out and back on th' shelves. Got some busted shelves, counters, too. Gonna cost money to make new ones."

"Naturally," Captain Ed said quietly. "Put it on my bill."

"Puttin' it on your bill, the whole works, counters, shelves, time," Karlson ran on as if he hadn't heard Captain Ed. "Puttin' it on right along with that $15,000 you owe me for the boat, plus your gas, oil, and grub. A hundred dollars, that's what it'll cost to clean up this mess and build new counters and shelves."

Captain Ed scrubbed a big hand across his face and looked at Karlson steadily. "Not a hundred." His voice was even. "I'll go fifty. Not one cent more."

Karlson opened his mouth to argue, then thought better of it. "Oh, all right. Fifty. But it won't pay for all of it, I'm tellin' you."

Karlson pointed a stubby finger at Brad and said: "You keep that mutt of yours on a rope or somethin' when you're around here, understand? I catch him runnin' loose just once and I'll let Duke take him. You hear me?"

As though on signal Duke lowered his big head and growled menacingly at Mickie.

Mickie growled back. Brad wrapped both arms around

93

Mickie's neck and looked fearfully at Duke. He was a dirty brown short-haired dog. He was much taller and heavier than Mickie. He had a head like a bulldog, with broad, powerful jaws. His chest was deep, his frame heavy-boned and muscular. He looked mean and vicious with those long tearing teeth sticking out on either side of his protruding jaws. He looked like a dog who loved to fight and kill.

"He's killed four dogs in town already," Karlson said with a touch of pride. "You'd better make sure yours ain't Number Five."

"Yes, sir," Brad said. "I'll keep him tied."

With that, Karlson went stamping off through the store, shouting, "Come on, Duke. Come on." Duke tossed a final growl at Mickie and trotted after Karlson.

Once outside, George muttered angrily: "I'd like to wring that fat runt's neck. A hundred dollars? Even fifty. One day and twenty dollars will put the whole shebang back in shape."

"I know," Captain Ed agreed. "But we're hardly in a position to argue much." He glanced down at Brad, and added, "You'd better believe what he said about turning Duke loose on Mickie."

"I do." Brad felt a stab of fear as he thought of the vicious-looking Duke. "I do."

As they went down the dock toward the stairs, Brad glanced up. The black cat was taking no chances. He was still perched on top of the piling.

six

They anchored for the night in a small bay several hours out of Orca City. They'd been watching for jumpers all the way, but had seen very few. As they ate supper in the galley, George observed, "Not many jumpers. The run seems pretty light."

"I *have* seen a lot more jumpers at the beginning of the season," Captain Ed agreed. "But wait till we hit Boulder Bay. If they're running anyplace, it'll be there."

"Why Boulder Bay?" Brad asked.

"A big stream comes in there, and thousands of salmon go up it to spawn. Get into fish heading for that stream and you're going to get a load."

They turned in early because the season opened at 6:00 A.M. the next morning. "I want to be ready to rake in our first load by 6:01," Captain Ed said. "We've got to be moving by five."

It was the first night Brad and Mickie had ever spent

aboard the boat. In spite of the opened ports, the heat of the engine and the thick odor of burned oil lay trapped in the compartment. Brad was not used to the hard, narrow bunk with the four-inch rail to keep one from rolling out in rough weather or to the knowledge that the sea was just two inches from his head on the opposite side of the planking. The *Annie B* rocked gently on the bosom of the sea, and Brad felt the slight tug as she came up against the holding anchor.

Mickie's delicate nostrils and thick fur could not stand the closeness of the compartment. He preferred the seine pile in the stern and the cool, fresh air of the open deck. But there he was alone, and he wanted to be with Brad. So he spent his time clicking back and forth, enduring each place as long as possible. Finally the open ports funneled sufficient night air into the compartment to cool and freshen it, and Mickie came down and flopped with a tired sigh on the deck at Brad's head.

Brad smiled in the dark, trailed a hand over the side, and twisted his fingers in Mickie's fur. He soon dropped off to sleep.

When he awoke, Mickie was gone and George was grinning down at him. "If you want breakfast you'd better roll out, Champ. This's the day we go to work."

Breakfast over, they began slowly cruising across the flat sea. George and Brad were on top of the wheelhouse spotting. Mickie leaned over the bow and stared into the clear water as if he, too, were searching.

"If we spot a school," George explained, "we'll just stay with it until six, then gather it in."

The early-morning breeze was gradually warmed by the

climbing sun until it became hot. Sunrays bounced off the water, and Brad had to squint his eyes almost shut to see. Flocks of sea parrots skimmed over the sea ahead of the *Annie B*, waited until the boat caught up, then flew ahead again. A whale curved out of the depths and in again with a disdainful flirt of his great tail. A porpoise came out of nowhere, cut slashing strokes inches before the cleaving bow, and disappeared.

Shortly after noon they passed the mouth of a long bay that nestled deep in the sheer folds of a towering mountain. Far back Brad made out the white ribbon of a large stream spilling into the sea. The mouth of the bay was guarded by a great mass of huge rocks that had been worn glass smooth over the centuries. A herd of sea lions lay dozing like huge brown slugs on the narrow beach and among the rocks. The *Annie B* was cruising by several hundred yards offshore when an old bull reared his great shoulders and gave voice to a hoarse roar of alarm. The next moment hundreds of sea lions were humping and bumping over the rocks and across the sand and plunging into the sea. They charged toward the *Annie B*, the sea boiling with their numbers, mouths open wide, snorting and bellowing menacingly. They came out a hundred yards or so, then began milling about as if undecided. Finally they turned and started back toward shore. Mickie leaned over the rail and barked at them at the top of his lungs.

Captain Ed thrust his black head out of the wheelhouse window and shouted up: "Boulder Bay! Now we go to work. Keep your eyes peeled."

"Why are there so many sea lions right here?" Brad asked.

97

"They know, as well as we do, that that stream emptying into the bay is one of the best spawning streams in the Sound," George answered. "They're here for the same reason we are. Salmon."

The afternoon hours wore on. They spotted a few jumpers and made three sets, but their total was less than a thousand fish in the hold.

"Practice for you," George said, and grinned at Brad. "Now you'll know what to do when we really get into 'em." Brad had learned how to pull the seine, fold it back on the turntable, ready to be run out without tangling or bunching for the next set. He handled the brail. The big dipnet operated from the boom aboard the boat. It could lift one hundred fish at a time. Brad steered it over the hold while Captain Ed worked the winch.

Mickie got into trouble the first two times. The moment fish began coming aboard, flopping and squirming, he dashed about barking and snapping at them through the mesh of the brail. Brad drove him into the galley, boxed his ears, and ordered him to stay there. The third time he did. But he whined and barked excitedly throughout the whole operation.

They were almost back to Boulder Bay. The sun was sliding down a red sky when they hit the big one.

Brad was alone on top the wheelhouse when he saw jumpers ahead. By the time he had yelled, "Jumpers ahead!" they were all about the *Annie B*. Captain Ed let out a whoop. George dashed aft, tumbled into the skiff with the end of the seine, and started the outboard motor. A minute later they had circled the school. When they pulled the net in close and

Brad looked down into the pocket, he was startled at the mass of salmon. There were more fish than water.

Captain Ed laughed delightedly and slapped Brad's back. "Good old Boulder Bay! She never lets us down."

Brad was glad now they'd made the previous sets. He was too busy to be learning what to do. When the first brail rose bulging with salmon, Mickie could no longer stand the excitement that had communicated itself to him. He dashed from the galley and attacked the brail, barking and growling and yanking on the mesh.

Brad yelled, "Get away from there, Mickie. Get!"

Captain Ed shouted, "Get that fool out of here before he rips the brail!"

Brad grabbed for Mickie. Captain Ed set the brake on the winch and came to help. The brake slipped, the brail crashed to the deck, and salmon were spewed in all directions. Brad got hold of Mickie, shoved him into the galley, and slammed the door. Mickie lunged at the door, clawing and barking wildly. Finally he began to howl.

George came up, and the three of them gathered up the flopping salmon and threw them into the hold. Ten minutes later they were brailing again.

This time it was hard work. The brail was heavy and unwieldy, holding more than five hundred pounds of salmon at a time. It took all Brad's strength to guide it over the open hatch and hold it steady while Captain Ed lowered it through the narrow opening. Icy water cascaded over him, and in minutes he was soaked. He didn't know how long the job took, but his arms and shoulders were aching and the muscles in his back and legs were jumping with weariness

99

when the pocket was empty. The hold was almost full. The sun had fallen into a blood-red sea, and Mickie was still howling at the top of his lungs.

Brad let Mickie out, and he raced about the deck, searching for the earlier excitement. When he found none he became quiet and lay down on the seine pile. They washed down the deck, put the hatch covers on, and swung the brail and boom against the mast.

"A good load," Captain Ed said happily. "A fine beginning. You'd better change clothes. You're soaked."

"Are we going in to the cannery tonight?" Brad asked.

"It won't be open, so we can't unload before morning. We'll pull down the coast a couple of miles, drop anchor, and get something to eat and a little rest. We'll pull out about one or two. That'll bring us to the cannery around eight."

With the experience of old sailors, Captain Ed and George were asleep almost immediately. Brad was sure he would be, too. But he had scarcely lain down when his hands began to burn. Pulling the seine and handling the heavy brail with his hands in sea water hours at a time had worn his skin thin, exactly like a rope burn.

It soon became more than he could stand, and followed by Mickie, he rose and went into the galley. He pumped a pan of cold water, sat at the table, and thrust both hands into the pan. The burning stopped. He sat there, holding his hands in the water, and looked out the open door at the dark, mysterious sea. A faint breeze, laced with the fresh, musty

It took all Brad's strength to guide it over the open hatch and hold it steady.

scent of the tundra, filled the galley. The sea was calm, and the undertones of the night came softly to him. The old-man face of a seal rose out of the depths so close Brad could see its big round eyes. Boy and seal stared at each other a long moment. Then the head disappeared without leaving a ripple.

Brad leaned forward on the table and closed his eyes, but kept his hands in the water. He was sitting there, half asleep, when Captain Ed came into the galley. He was barefoot and wore only his pants. He lighted the lamp and examined Brad's hands. "You should have woke me," he said. "In fact, I should have checked your hands. Mine got that way at first." He went to the cupboard and took down the lard pail. "Dry your hands good."

After Brad had dried his hands, Captain Ed scooped out a pat of lard and put it in his palms. "Rub it around until it melts and soaks into the skin. It'll stop the burning."

They sat opposite each other, and the lamp shone on Captain Ed's jet-black hair and threw lights and shadows across the lean hardness of his chest and shoulders. The burning began to leave Brad's palms.

Captain Ed said: "Today gave you a fair sample of what seining's like. How'd you like it?"

"I liked it fine. Did I do my share? Did I hold up my end as good as a man would?"

"You sure did."

"You wouldn't just say that?"

"I don't have to." Captain Ed touched Brad's palms. "You want proof, there it is."

103

"I'm glad. I was kind of worried. But Mickie did cause trouble. He got in the way and he almost ruined the brail."

"But he didn't." Captain Ed smiled. "He was excited. After this, we'll lock him in every time we begin to brail."

"And yesterday he tore up the store. That cost you fifty dollars and made Mr. Karlson pretty mad."

"That fifty dollars won't break us, and Karlson is usually mad about something. We'll just keep Mickie out of the store from now on. Stop worrying, son. The important thing is, you handled a man's job today." Captain Ed looked at his own hands folded on the table, and said thoughtfully, "Give you a few years working with George and me, and you'll be ready for your own boat."

"I'd sure like that."

Captain Ed kept looking at his hands. "No reason we can't think about it; plan on it, even. In four or five years, with any kind of luck, we can save enough with the *Annie B* to buy another boat. You and George could skipper the next one. I'd get some pickup men for the *Annie B*. We wouldn't buy just any old boat. We'd look and look until we found another *Annie B*." He smiled at Brad, his black eyes shining, "Be something, two *Annie B*'s in the family."

"You really mean it?" Brad was breathless with the thought.

"Been thinking of it for some time. I had to be sure you liked seining first."

"A boat like the *Annie B* costs a lot of money," Brad said doubtfully. "Do you really think we could do it, Captain Ed?"

"Of course. We'll all work at it: you, George, Annie, and me. A family can do anything, once it sets its mind to it."

"I know," Brad agreed. The gray eyes of the boy and the snapping black eyes of the man met, and they smiled at each other in complete understanding.

"How're the hands?"

"They're fine now."

"Then let's get some sleep. We'll have to pull out in another four hours."

When they arrived at the cannery next morning, one seiner was unloading and several others were gassing up. "I see they've got a few," George observed.

When their turn came and they pulled under the conveyor, Captain Ed said to Brad: "We'll unload. You can look around if you like. And go up to the store for your shirts. Put the collar on Mickie, and don't let him inside."

Mickie was anxious to get ashore again, and half dragged Brad up the stairs to the dock.

Brad had never seen fish unloaded or been through a cannery. He climbed the walkway to the conveyor and watched Captain Ed and George pewing fish onto the conveyor belt. The fish counter stood almost above Brad, tallying the salmon with an automatic counting device. Brad became interested watching the man, and moved nearer. The tallyman noticed him, and yelled, "Hey, kid, get outa here! You've got no business up here. Go on, beat it!"

Brad and Mickie went back down the steps and followed the conveyor belt inside the cannery.

The inside was spotlessly clean. Before him were a dozen

or so big fish bins. Several were full, a couple partially filled. The conveyor was running their catch into an empty bin. Before him a black machine banged and clattered. A line of empty cans clicked in one end and emerged filled with salmon out the other. Brad knew this machine was called the "Iron Chink." Girls stationed along the line checked the cans to make sure they were filled. The cans marched into a second machine from which they emerged sealed. Farther down, men were shoving racks of canned salmon into a great steel tube for cooking. Even as he watched, they slammed the door and bolted it shut. Steam began to feather out around the edge.

He went back out the way he'd entered. Captain Ed and George were still tossing a silvery stream of fish onto the conveyor. He stopped and watched the fish counter for several minutes. Finally he and Mickie wandered on down the dock to the end of the cannery building and the store. He tied Mickie to a cleat on the dock and went inside.

The black cat was curled up asleep on the same counter. The store had been cleaned up. Charlie Frost came down the aisle grinning. "Look a little different than last time?"

"Sure does," Brad agreed.

"Where's th' wolf?"

"I left him tied outside."

Charlie nodded. "I guess you want your shirts?"

"Yes, I'd like two."

Charlie began rummaging through piles of shirts. "Didn't know Ed and Annie had a boy relative."

"I'm not really a relative. I'm Brad Nichols."

Charlie looked up, "Fred Nichols' boy? I knew your dad."

He picked up a shirt and held it against Brad. " 'Bout right in the chest and shoulders. Arms are kinda short, though."

"I've got to have the arms long enough."

"Here's a size bigger." Charlie draped another shirt against Brad's chest. "Arms 'bout right, I'd say. Little big through th' chest an' shoulders, though, but you'll fill that out. I'd say this's 'bout it." While he wrapped the shirts, Charlie asked, "How do you like livin' with th' Bishops an' George?"

"Just fine," Brad said, and took his shirts and left.

The moment he stepped out the door he saw Duke standing a few feet off, glaring at Mickie. His thick legs were braced and his heavy lips were lifted, exposing the big tearing teeth. A growl was rumbling from the depths of his broad chest.

Mickie crouched at the end of his chain, head down, eyes narrowed, and every tooth shining. He matched Duke growl for growl. Brad could not understand why Mickie was not afraid. Now that he saw them together again, he realized how big Duke really was. He was inches taller than Mickie; his chest was broader, deeper, his frame more powerful. He outweighed Mickie many pounds, and all of it was bulging muscle. And he had those terrible teeth.

Duke began advancing a slow, stiff-legged step at a time. Brad looked about frantically. A broken piece of board from one of the counters lay nearby. He grabbed it and yelled at Duke, "Get back! You get back!"

Duke looked at the club. He knew what it meant, and stopped. But he did not back away. He stood just beyond reach, small eyes watching the club in Brad's hands.

Brad untied Mickie's chain. He held it and his shirts in

107

one hand, the menacing club in the other, and started down the dock toward the stairs. Mickie held back, facing Duke, ready to fight. Brad yanked on the chain. "Come on. Come on." He was angry at Mickie, and frightened, too. "Quit that! He's too big for you. You want to get killed? Come on, Mickie!"

Duke followed all the way to the stairs. The only thing that kept him from attacking Mickie was the sight of the club. Brad kept yanking on the chain and talking to Mickie, trying to distract his attention from Duke. "You must be crazy," he said. "He's lots bigger and stronger than you are. You can't fight him. He'll kill you. You want to get torn to pieces, you darned fool?"

Duke stopped following at the top of the stairs, but he watched them all the way to the bottom and along the float to the *Annie B.*

When they stepped aboard, Captain Ed and George were tossing the last of the salmon onto the conveyor. Captain Ed saw the stick, then glanced up and saw Duke on the dock.

"He followed us all the way from the store," Brad said. "He wanted to fight Mickie, but he's afraid of a stick."

"Then keep it handy. Duke's too much dog for Mickie."

"What kind of dog is he?"

George wiped his sweating face with a handkerchief and said: "About four kinds, I'd guess. And all big and mean."

"Why would anybody want a dog like Duke?" Brad wondered.

"Protection," George said promptly. "Karlson's pulled some pretty raw deals on seiners. He's been threatened plenty of times. But who wants to take a punch at the fat little runt with Duke around."

"Could be," Captain Ed agreed. "Duke's always with him."

They replaced the hatch covers, and Captain Ed said: "I'll get our ticket and we'll head out. I'll bet this was the biggest load they've had so far."

Brad, Mickie, and George were in the galley, and Brad was wearing one of the new shirts when Captain Ed returned. He asked George, "How many do you figure we had?"

"They told us she'd carry ten thousand. We were pretty near full. I'd say around nine thousand."

"That's what I thought." Captain Ed handed George the ticket.

"Seventy-two hundred! Oh, no, I don't go for this." George looked at Captain Ed. "We've heard of his cute little tricks. But he never tried 'em on us before."

"He has now. I'd guess we were short-counted at least fifteen hundred. But we can't prove it against the counter."

Brad asked, "Is he supposed to press the button on that thing he holds in his hand every time a fish goes by?"

Captain Ed nodded. "That's right."

"He didn't. I watched him. Lots of times two or three fish went by, but he only pressed it once. I wasn't sure the first time. I went inside the cannery, and when I came out I watched him again. I know he didn't press it every time."

"Oldest trick in the business," George scowled.

"Hard to prove."

109

"Don't have to prove it." George stretched his huge arms, arched his big chest, and took a hitch in his pants. "This's my department." He turned to Brad, "You know which bin our fish went in?"

"I can show you."

"Come on. Skipper, don't move the boat so anyone else can get in to unload until we get back."

"Don't get in any trouble over this," Captain Ed warned.

George smiled, but his voice had an ugly edge: "You're worrying over the wrong man. Come on, Champ."

They went into the cannery building, and Brad pointed out the bin that held the *Annie B*'s fish. The bin was almost full. "You're sure this bin was empty when they started running ours in?"

"I came up here almost as soon as you and Captain Ed began tossing them on the conveyor. The bottom of the bin wasn't covered yet."

"That's good enough. Come on. And, Champ, you make like a mouse when we get in the office. Don't say a word unless I ask you. And do whatever I say."

"What're you going to do?" Brad asked, his heart beginning to pound.

"Scare the runt out of a year's growth if I can," George said grimly.

When they walked into the office, Frank Karlson's small figure was hunched at an old roll-top desk behind a railing that blocked off the desk from the rest of the room. Duke stood just inside the door.

George left the door open. Then, with a speed that startled Brad, George took one long step, clamped a big hand on the loose hide behind Duke's neck, the other on his back, lifted and tossed the dog outside and slammed the door. It was done so quickly the startled Duke didn't even have time to growl. The next instant he hit the closed door, growling and tearing at it.

Karlson swung around just in time to stare up into the broad, scowling face of George leaning over the railing. George dropped the ticket on the desk and said, "Look at it."

Karlson glanced at the ticket, then up at George. "What about it?" he said in his file-on-metal voice.

"I won't take this count," George said calmly. "It's short."

"Not according to the ticket." Karlson slapped the ticket with a pudgy hand. "I go by the ticket."

"Not this time. Our fish are in a separate bin. We'll count 'em over if necessary."

"Those fish belong to me," Karlson flared. "You don't touch 'em. If Ed Bishop thinks he can run a fast one like this on me, he's crazy."

"The Skipper's out of this one," George said. "This's me. I get a share of this catch, and I don't let some cheap little runt cheat me."

"Why, you big dumb ox," Karlson's little pot belly began to bounce and his fat cheeks· turned red, "I'll have th' marshal down here. I'll— Hey . . . !"

With the same speed he had used in ousting Duke, George leaned across the railing, clamped big hands on Karlson, heaved and lifted him bodily, squirming and kicking, over the rail. He set Karlson on his feet, kept both hands clamped on him, and glared down at the cannery owner. He

111

towered over the little man. George's lumpy brows were drawn together in a fierce scowl; his big, scarred face with its blunt jaw was thrust out belligerently. This was not the kindly, gentle George Brad had known. This George was tough, threatening. He looked like the man who had once almost fought for the heavyweight championship of the world. Even his voice was an ugly, menacing growl that sounded as dangerous as Duke's. "That's a good idea. I'll send the boy for the marshal. It'll take about fifteen minutes for him to get here. That time you're going to spend with me, little man." He grinned mirthlessly at Karlson. "It's going to be the longest, toughest, hardest fifteen minutes you'll ever spend in your life."

"You—you'll go to jail," Karlson sputtered.

"Naturally." George gave the little man an ugly smile. "But that won't help you. Not where you're going to be for the next couple of months. And right during the canning season, too."

"You're crazy! Crazy as a loon!" Karlson wriggled frantically to get loose. He was as firmly held as if by a vise.

"You'll see," George said with fatalistic calm. "I'm an expert at this sort of thing. Remember? Champ," he said, without taking his baleful look from Karlson, "go get the marshal. And try to be back in fifteen minutes. Not before. Understand?"

"Yes," Brad turned toward the door.

"Wait!" Karlson bleated. "Wait. What d'you want?"

"I'll settle for eighty-five hundred on this ticket. Not one less."

"Eighty-five hundred! You're robbin' me."

George lifted Karlson and shook him until his heels snapped. "Get the marshal, Champ," he said to Brad. "Get going."

"No! No! Wait!" Karlson chattered. "All right. Eighty-five hundred."

Karlson took the ticket, wrote in the desired amount, and handed it to George.

"Initial it," George ordered.

Karlson did.

George dropped the ticket in his pocket. "We'll be going now. When I open the door Duke'll be coming in. You make sure he don't do anything, if you want to keep him alive. Understand?"

Karlson nodded. "Get out," he croaked. "Get out."

"Of course," George said. "Of course." He opened the door and Duke stalked in, glaring first at George and then at Brad.

Karlson muttered hoarsely, "Come here, Duke. Come here."

George and Brad went out and down the dock and aboard the *Annie B.* George dropped the ticket on the galley table and Captain Ed looked at it. "Eighty-five hundred. That's more like it. I'll settle for that. How'd you do it?"

"I just reasoned with him," George said easily. "You know, maybe we've got him all wrong. He's a right reasonable man—once he understands. That right, Champ?"

"Yes, sir," Brad agreed.

Captain Ed looked George up and down, his black eyes twinkling. "I can imagine," he murmured. "I can just imagine."

113

seven

An hour later they were headed back over the same route toward Boulder Bay. They were less than three hours from the cannery when they spotted a school of jumpers and ran out the seine. They worked the trapped school in close and looked down into the pocket. It was not so big as the first load, but it was well worth the effort.

Brad shoved a protesting Mickie into the galley and closed the door and they began brailing. Mickie whined, scratched on the door, and finally went to howling. He howled all through the operation. When they finished, Brad let him out; he rushed to the open hatches and stared down at the mass of salmon with Captain Ed, George, and Brad. "About six thousand," Captain Ed said happily. "That makes two loads in less than twenty-four hours. Not bad. It looks like the Bureau of Fisheries was right when they predicted a big run. We'd better head right back to the cannery with these.

You're getting pretty good," he said, and smiled at Brad. "You didn't get soaked this time. How's the hands?"

"They only sting a little."

"Put some more lard on 'em. By tomorrow you won't feel a thing."

They pulled in to the cannery late that afternoon. There were no seiners unloading and only two at the gas dock. They eased up under the conveyor and got the hatches off. While Captain Ed and George pewed salmon onto the conveyor belt, Brad put the collar and chain on Mickie to take him up on the dock for exercise.

They went along the float and up the stairs. Mickie strained against the chain. He wanted to run. They had barely gained the dock when Duke trotted around a far corner of the cannery building. The moment he saw Mickie he came galloping toward them. Brad hadn't brought the stick because he'd planned to walk Mickie at the far outer edge of the dock, well away from Duke's domain. But here he was. Brad looked about for some weapon. There was no stick, nothing to fend Duke off with. He began backing hurriedly toward the stairs, dragging Mickie with him.

They had barely started down when Duke pulled up at the top. As before, he did not follow them down, but stood at the edge, glared down at them, and began to growl.

A dozen steps down, Mickie lunged at the chain and matched Duke growl for growl. He was not awed by Duke's size and fierce looks. Brad yanked him down the stairs to the float and there he put his arms around Mickie's neck. Mickie continued to look up the stairs at Duke, and growl.

Brad cuffed his ears and said, "Cut that out!" Mickie looked at him, surprised, then quit growling. Brad put his face against Mickie's forehead, and said: "Why don't you get smart? You know he's too big and tough for you. Even Captain Ed says so. He's killed four dogs already. He knows how to fight. You've never had a fight in your life. I don't want you killed."

Mickie licked his face, and grinned.

Mickie needed exercise, but Duke blocked the way at the head of the stairs. Brad thought of getting the club and climbing to the dock again. Duke would respect the club. But he knew Duke would follow just beyond the club's reach, waiting his chance to spring upon Mickie. He couldn't watch both dogs every second. Sooner or later Duke would see his chance, and that would be the end of Mickie. The only place left for exercising Mickie was the hundred yards of float where they stood.

Brad walked Mickie up and down the float, and Duke kept pace with them on the dock above, growling his threats. The big dog kept up his vigil until Captain Ed and George had unloaded the salmon and they were heading back to sea.

Captain Ed scowled at Duke and shook his head. "Ugly brute, but we can't do a thing about it now. Soon as we get Karlson paid off, we'll take our fish elsewhere."

"That won't be this season."

"I'm afraid not." Captain Ed patted Mickie's head. "You two will have to sweat it out."

"We can. Where are we heading now?"

"Right back toward Boulder Bay. Never forsake your luck."

This time they spotted no promising numbers of jumpers, and they finally anchored for the night in a cove an hour's run from Boulder Bay.

Next morning they were out early, boring along the coast on a sharp lookout for a set. Fog banners hung in wide-spaced streamers across the sea, but the climbing sun soon burned them away. The sea lay utterly flat and bounced the sun off the water. It made Brad squint as he searched for jumpers. The *Annie B* finally came opposite the rock-bound entrance to Boulder Bay, perhaps a quarter mile offshore. Brad could see the sluglike shapes of sea lions sunning themselves on the rocks and the heads of dozens of others bobbing about in the water. The sounds of their bellowing and snorting were an endless din drifting across the sea.

Then he sighted the jumpers straight ahead and let out a yell. Captain Ed's voice sounded at the same instant. George ran, and tumbled into the skiff. The outboard roared, and the seine began sliding smoothly off the stern into the sea. Brad shoved Mickie into the galley again and closed the door.

In moments they had the school surrounded and began pinching in the seine. When they finally looked down into the pocket, it was boiling with salmon.

"A big one!" Captain Ed grinned at Brad. "What did I tell you about never forsaking your luck?"

They were still looking into the pocket when Brad saw the head of a sea lion rise out of the water not ten feet from the seine. Then another, and another. Suddenly they were popping up all around the *Annie B*, their big eyes fastened on the pocket and the huge school of salmon churning there.

George yelled, "Sea lions!" dived for the galley, and returned with the rifle. Captain Ed grabbed the pike pole off the top of the wheelhouse.

As though on signal, the army of sea lions charged the seine to get at the trapped salmon. To Brad it was as if a madness had seized the herd. They came bellowing, mouths wide, churning the sea to foam. Huge bodies, weighing as much as a thousand pounds, hurtled into the net, wicked teeth cutting and slashing with wild abandon.

The rifle began to explode. Captain Ed used the pike pole like a spear, driving the sharp point up to the barb into their huge bodies.

Brad looked about frantically for a weapon. There was nothing on deck. But in the bottom of the skiff was an oar kept there for emergencies if the outboard motor failed. He jumped into the skiff, snatched up the oar, and began flailing at the sea lions. Suddenly Mickie was on deck, leaning over the rail, barking and snarling down at the sea lions. George had left the galley door open when he ran for the rifle, and Mickie was adding his voice to the uproar.

Brad whacked a sea lion over the back, but the animal didn't even seem to know he'd been hit. Another surfaced beside the skiff, and Brad brought the oar down on its head with all his strength. The animal sank, came up six feet away, and plunged on. The water turned red with the dead and dying. But the rifle, the pike pole, and Brad's flailing oar could not stop them. In their mad frenzy to get at the trapped salmon they poured over their own dead and injured in a brown wave and charged into the seine. In seconds the seine was torn to shreds and the frightened salmon had escaped back to sea with the sea lions in hot pursuit.

As suddenly as it had begun, it was over. Sweat streamed down Captain Ed's face as he leaned tiredly on the pike pole. George pumped the last empty shell from the rifle and just stood there. Brad laid down the oar and climbed back aboard. The shredded seine drifted, held up by the floats. Once again the sea was quiet. The only sound was the busy *click-click* of Mickie's claws as he trotted back and forth, peering over the side, looking for something to bark at.

They hauled in the damaged seine, inspecting it carefully as it came aboard. When it was all on the turntable, Captain Ed shook his head. "That's as good a job of destruction as I've ever seen. This seine's a total loss." He sat down heavily on the rail and ran a hand through his black hair. For a little while they were all quiet, overcome by the suddenness of the tragedy. Finally Captain Ed said: "We haven't time to make another. We've got to rustle up a spare seine somewhere. Where's a good place to look?"

"That's like looking for hen's teeth," George said.

"You mean, we might not find one?" Brad asked.

Captain Ed nodded. "Most everybody makes his own. That's why there's never any lying around to buy. We always made ours, but it's a long, slow job."

"We can't work without a seine," Brad was thinking aloud. "And if we can't work, we can't pay Karlson."

"Exactly. Every year a lot of seiners get caught in some such jam. I never figured I would. And while we're on the subject, you took an awful chance jumping into the skiff and whaling those sea lions with the oar. They might have tipped the skiff over, and then you'd have been in the sea with them. They'd have chewed you up plenty, maybe killed you

119

before we could have got you out. Don't ever do a thing like that again."

"I didn't think. They were ruining our seine, and you and George were fighting them. I had to do something."

"You did plenty."

"I just remembered something." George thumbed his hat onto the back of his head. "Remember Johnny Noble? He owed Orca City Cannery money last fall, and Karlson confiscated his seine for payment. I seem to remember seeing it piled in the cannery loft. And that was practically a new seine."

Captain Ed heaved himself erect. "Let's go see if it's still there. You fellows keep your fingers crossed."

They made the Orca City Cannery late in the afternoon and tied up to the float below the dock. Captain Ed said to Brad: "Better come along. It'll take all of us to get it out of the loft, if it's there."

They locked Mickie in the galley and left him protesting loudly. While Captain Ed and George went to the office to see Karlson, Brad wandered along the cannery dock and stopped to look in the big open end of the building.

He was standing there, watching the cans of salmon spitting out the end of the Iron Chink, when a cold nose touched his hand. Mickie was grinning up at him, his tail waving happily.

Brad glanced fearfully about, but Duke was not in sight. "Come on," he said quickly. "Let's get out of here. How did you get out of the galley?"

Mickie trotted beside him as he hurried toward the stairs. They had almost reached them when Duke trotted into sight, coming from the direction of the office. He spotted Mickie immediately and came on at his stiff-legged, heavy-footed gallop. He stopped a few feet off, big head down, his legs braced. A growl rumbled from his chest, and his heavy lips lifted away from the long teeth. He was blocking their escape to the stairs, and he seemed to know it.

Brad looked about frantically for a stick or a piece of wood with which to bluff Duke. There was nothing. Mickie was answering Duke growl for growl. Brad twisted a hand in the long fur of his neck and held Mickie back. He yelled at Duke, "Get out of here! Go on, beat it!" He raised his free arm and made threatening, throwing motions.

Duke was not bluffed. He kept his eyes on Mickie, and advanced a slow step.

Brad tried to back away. He tried to drag Mickie with him. "Come on!" He yanked on Mickie's fur. "Come on, Mickie!" he yelled frantically. "Come on!"

But this time Mickie refused to budge. He stood, wolflike head lowered, eyes narrowed, watching Duke. Mickie had stopped growling, and Brad could feel the spring-like tensing of his muscles. Brad realized then what Mickie had known from the first moment: There was no running away this time.

Brad took his hand from Mickie's neck and began backing away. He wanted his dog to have complete freedom of movement. If Mickie could hold Duke off for even a minute, that would give him time to run to the cannery office and get George and Captain Ed. Maybe they could save Mickie from being killed.

Duke came on confidently. His whole air said that here

was a fighter, a killer who knew exactly what he meant to do.

The fight exploded in full fury with a suddenness that caught Brad unprepared. He just stood there rooted to the dock, eyes wide with horrified fascination.

Duke rushed with a thunderous growl, big jaws snapping like a steel trap at Mickie's throat. But Mickie was not there. He had leaped lightly away, then in. His teeth flashed, and one of Duke's ears was slashed to ribbons. Duke whirled and charged, bellowing with rage. Mickie avoided the rush, leaped in again, slashed Duke's shoulder to the bone, and was again beyond reach. He enveloped Duke in a whirlwind of rushes and feints. He was in and out, slashing and ripping. He soon had Duke bleeding from half a dozen deep cuts but was himself untouched.

Brad was amazed, but as he watched he began to understand. Duke had always fought the smaller, softer town dogs. He could corner them and overwhelm them with his size and strength. Against Mickie he was slow and ponderous, his bulging muscles and great strength useless against the other's speed. Brad remembered stories he'd heard of how wolves fought, leaping in and out, teeth flashing like razors. The wolf in Mickie was fighting Duke. It was not something he had needed to learn by meeting other dogs. This had been bred into his kind with the first cross between a gray arctic wolf and an Eskimo dog ages ago, and came down through countless generations of Malamutes. Here was a murderous combination of the tough northern dog's strength, and the lightning speed, cunning, and endurance of a wolf. Poor clumsy, slow Duke was unable to cope with such a way of fighting.

Noise of the fight carried inside the cannery. A man appeared, took one look, and let out a shout. In seconds, machines were shut down and the whole cannery crew streamed out and surrounded the fighters. Men and women began yelling for Mickie. "Come on, wolf. Eat 'im up! Kill the ugly devil! Kill 'im!"

Mickie was in a fair way of doing just that. He was all over Duke, slashing and tearing, leaping in and out, evading and eluding, only to leap in again, punish Duke, and escape unscathed.

Duke had spent his whole life in and around the cannery, and was not toughened for a long fight. The stamina that could keep a wolf on a hunting trail for days on end had not been bred into him as it had into Mickie. Duke tired fast. His growls and snarls were as blood-chilling as ever. But now when he rushed and Mickie sprang lightly aside, Duke almost fell trying to turn and follow. In sheer desperation he charged Mickie full tilt, big head swinging, jaws reaching as Mickie leaped away. Duke tried to stop and turn. At that moment he was completely off balance, and Mickie's solid hundred pounds hurtled against him, shoulder meeting shoulder squarely. Duke was knocked rolling. Mickie drove straight for the throat, where instinct told him life pulsed close to the surface. So quick was his charge and so fast were they fighting, that their momentum carried them to the edge of the dock, where, growling and slashing, they toppled off the edge and fell into the sea.

Brad rushed to the rail with the cannery crew. Both dogs had surfaced, and Duke was splashing frantically toward the float a few feet off. The fight was knocked completely out of him. His head was up and his eyes were fixed on the float as he strained toward it. Brad saw with surprise that Duke could barely swim. That was the reason he hadn't followed them down the stairs yesterday. Duke was afraid of the water.

Not so with Mickie. He was swimming strongly, and even in the sea he was still carrying the fight to Duke. He literally swam on top of the struggling Duke, grabbed the back of his neck, and rode him under. Duke shook free, came up coughing and choking and paddling wildly. Mickie was after him and rode him under again.

Then Brad saw George plunge down the stairs and race along the float. He was followed by Captain Ed and a waddling Karlson. Brad came out of his shocked trance and rushed for the stairs, too.

When he reached the end of the float George had already jerked both dogs from the sea. Duke lay on the float, half drowned and bleeding from a dozen gashes. Karlson and George were bending over, inspecting him. Captain Ed had both arms around the dripping Mickie. Mickie, the fight still raging within him, was squirming and growling, trying to get loose to pounce on the helpless Duke.

Captain Ed shoved Mickie at Brad. "Get him back aboard the boat. How'd he get loose?"

"I don't know," Brad said. "I was on the dock, and suddenly there he was. I was bringing him back to the boat, but Duke got in front of the stairs and wouldn't let us pass. Mickie had to fight."

Brad cuffed Mickie's ears and said sharply: "You stop that! Quit it! Hear!" He cuffed him again, hard, and finally the dog quit struggling. But he continued to growl. With a hand twisted in his wet fur, Brad dragged Mickie down the float and aboard the *Annie B.* The galley door was still closed, but the window above the table was open.

Inside the galley Brad looked Mickie over. He stood quiet and panting now, the fight boiled out of him. There were a few patches of hair missing where Duke's teeth had come close, and a nick on his shoulder oozed a few drops of blood. Otherwise the dog was untouched.

A few minutes later Frank Karlson went along the float leading a wobbly, badly beaten Duke.

Captain Ed and George came into the galley, and Brad pointed to the open window. "I opened it myself to air out the galley," Captain Ed said. He looked at Mickie closely. "Nothing wrong with you. I'd never have believed you could take Duke."

George squatted and took Mickie's head in his big hands and said: "You're a good fightin' man, Mick. You used your speed; you hit and run. You made the big muscle-bound lug wear himself out chasing you, while you picked him to pieces. You did just right. I'm mighty proud of you." Mickie lifted his lips in a grin and waved his tail happily, as if he understood what the high praise was all about.

Brad asked, "Is Duke going to be all right?"

Captain Ed nodded. "He looks like he'd been caught in a meat grinder and he's about half drowned, but otherwise he's okay."

"What about a seine?"

"Karlson's got one and it's for sale. We were just getting

down to serious talk about it when we heard the rumpus. We'd better get back there and make a deal," he said to George.

"You want me to go with you?"

"We'll come for you when we're ready. And," Captain Ed added as they started out, "close that window."

They returned in a few minutes, and Brad asked, "Do we go for the seine now?"

"Not yet." Captain Ed sat down at the galley table and stared at his hands thoughtfully. George leaned against the sink, his ragged brows pulled into a scowl Brad had come to recognize as anger.

"We can get it, can't we?"

"Sure, if we pay his price," George growled. "That cheap little punk! Someday I'll wring his fat neck, just as sure as shootin'."

"I know exactly what you mean." Captain Ed rose and started for the wheelhouse. "It's not far to Western Fisheries, and they've got a shortwave set. Let's go down there and call every cannery in the Sound and see if we can raise another seine."

Ten minutes later they were tying up at the Western Fisheries dock, and Captain Ed said to Brad, "You and Mickie hold down the fort while George and I see what we can find."

Brad and Mickie sat on the torn seine pile and watched the gulls. A cloud of them wheeled and dived over the offal chute. A row squatted along the cannery ridge. Gulls walked about the dock, squatted on piling ends and along the dock railing. A voice called from one boat to another, "Time to eat." The aroma of cooking food drifted across the water.

A little later George dropped down the ladder nailed to the face of the dock and stepped aboard. He shook his head at Brad, went into the galley, and sprawled on a bench. Brad and Mickie followed him, and George said: "We called every cannery in the Sound. Karlson's got the only seine around."

Brad sat down across the table from George, and Mickie leaned against his legs. Brad scratched the dog's ears and asked, "How much does Karlson want?"

"Twelve hundred."

"Doesn't a new one cost almost a thousand?"

"Karlson wants more than just money."

"What else?"

George studied the boy. He shifted his long legs uncomfortably. Then he said, "We get rid of Mickie or there's no seine at any price."

Brad's first reaction was to put a protective arm around Mickie. "Get rid of Mickie! Why?"

"Because of the fight and the lickin' Duke took."

Brad's lips were suddenly dry. "What—what did Captain Ed say?"

"He walked out."

Brad held Mickie close, and said: "Just because a couple of dogs get in a fight and his gets beat he wants to take it out on us. That doesn't make sense."

"Does when you know Karlson. He's got as much pride as if he was ten feet tall. Proud of his cannery, proud he can order people around, and especially proud of that brute of a

127

dog of his. Proud he killed four dogs. He's always bragging how big and tough Duke is. Then I come along and rough him up over that miscount on the fish. Before he can get over the humiliation of that, Mickie practically kills Duke, his pride and joy—and right in front of the whole cannery crew."

"But why get rid of Mickie? We can keep him aboard the boat when we're at the cannery."

George shook his head. "It's his way of getting even with us. The only way he knows he can fight back, and win."

"Where's Captain Ed now?"

"Asking around among the boats if anybody knows where there might be a spare seine."

"Do you think he might find one?"

"Don't bet on it, Champ."

"We've got to have a seine." Brad's arm tightened around Mickie and he drew the dog close. "Did—did Captain Ed say I'd have to get rid of Mickie?"

"He wouldn't say that. That's why he's looking so hard. If you were his real flesh and blood he might, and no matter how much you howled, that's how it'd be. But you're not."

"He said I was part of the family. So did Annie. And I am, George."

"Of course you are. And they couldn't think more of a real son. But you're still not a flesh-and-blood son, so Skipper doesn't feel he has the right to talk like a real father might."

Captain Ed came down the ladder and stepped aboard. Brad didn't ask if he'd found a seine. One look at his sober face told him. Captain Ed sat down on the bench beside Brad.

George asked, "Like we figured?"

"If there's an extra seine around, it's well hidden."

"Let's face it," George said. "There isn't."

Captain Ed looked at his hands folded on the tabletop, and said thoughtfully, "Wonder how long it'd take to make a seine, if we worked night and day?"

"Most of the season."

"I could help," Brad said. "Wouldn't that make it faster?"

"Some," George agreed, "but not near enough, Champ. The fish are running now. We've got to seine now."

"Maybe if we offered Karlson more money . . ." Captain Ed said.

"It's not extra money he wants. We know that."

Captain Ed said nothing, and for a little while there was silence in the small galley. Then George said: "Skipper, let's face it. There's one solution. Only one."

Captain Ed looked at George, and nodded. "Annie," he said. "We're going back and talk to Annie. She's just got to keep Mickie."

Brad thought of the months Annie had refused to touch Mickie, refused even to speak to him, her flat order to take him aboard the boat at the beginning of the season. He asked, "Do you think she'll take him, Skipper?"

"She's got to. We're in a jam." He heaved himself erect. "There's no sense losing more time waiting around here. Let's get going."

They ran all night. Captain Ed and George took turns at the wheel, and they arrived back at the little dock around noon. Smoke was roping from the chimney.

As they went up the trail, George said: "Man, I can almost smell it from here! Annie's making jam."

129

They rounded a corner of the cabin as Annie came to the door. She wore an apron over her jeans and had a huge spoon in her hand. "What brings you fellows home?" she asked in her gravelly voice. "You're supposed to be seining."

"We've got a problem," Captain Ed said. "Let's go inside."

Annie followed them in and stood in the middle of the room, fists on hips, waiting.

Mickie, who had never been allowed inside, stopped in the doorway and stood there, sharp ears pricked forward, looking in at them.

Annie listened while Captain Ed explained about losing the seine, Mickie's fight with Duke, and Karlson's refusal to sell them a seine unless they'd get rid of Mickie.

"Just the sort of cute trick you'd expect of Karlson," Annie said angrily. "So Mickie took that four-footed freak of a Duke? Good for him!"

"And bad for us," Captain Ed said, "with Karlson having the only seine around. We've got to get Mickie off the boat. It's crazy, but that's the way it is, the way Karlson is. And we need that seine right now. We've got two good loads in, and we had a third in the seine when the sea lions charged into it. We can't wait. The fish are running. You've got to keep Mickie so we can get that seine and go back to work."

Annie scowled at Captain Ed, chin outthrust, her lips set and uncompromising.

"The only other thing I can do is shoot Mickie or give him to some stranger. I'm darned if I'll do either one just to satisfy Karlson and that crazy phobia you've got about dogs. This is an emergency, Annie!"

Annie looked at Brad, then turned and looked at Mickie.

130

Mickie cocked his head and studied Annie as if he, too, waited.

Brad held his breath and watched Annie's rock-stubborn face. There was no break in her tough expression. But she finally said: "All right. Under the circumstances I guess I'll have to take him. We can't let Karlson beat us this way. Brad, go tie Mickie up again." As Brad went out the door and led Mickie to the doghouse, she asked, "You fellows want something to eat before you leave?"

"We can't take the time," Captain Ed said. "We've got to get back to Orca City and put that seine aboard and get to fishing. We've lost more than two days already."

131

eight

With the new seine aboard they again put to sea, but for some strange reason the run had stopped. The *Annie B* and more than a thousand other seiners ranged far and wide searching for the elusive salmon. They made set after set, but caught so few they barely paid the gas bill. The bulk of the salmon, if there were any left for a run this year, remained somewhere far at sea.

The giant brown bears ranged the creek banks, patiently searching for their favorite food in vain. Finally hunger drove them back to the meadows, to eating grass and roots and berries and ripping apart logs and stumps in their search for grubs and ants. Foxes, which haunt the streams along with the bears, returned to the brush patches and timber to hunt ground squirrels and mice. Eagles and hawks cruised endlessly over the streams, but finally soared inland in search of smaller game. Even the gulls, those scavengers who will grow fat where other birds and animals starve, were driven from the streams by the lack of food.

All across the Sound people and animals waited and watched and hoped for the return of the salmon. The annual run was their lifeblood, and it had dried up almost before it began. But the days wore on, and only a few stragglers entered the streams to spawn. Gloom settled over the industry and over the *Annie B* in particular, for not in years had such a complete stoppage been seen.

"It'll come," George said hopefully. "It can hit any hour. It can start again as quick as it stopped. We've just got to keep hoping and looking. The season's only a week old. We've still got plenty of time. Don't forget, the Bureau of Fisheries predicted this'd be a big year."

"I hope you and the Bureau are right," Captain Ed said. "But I've known of runs to come so late the season was over and they did no one any good. Let's hope it doesn't happen again."

Brad, too, was worried over the lack of a run. And he was worried about Mickie. He wondered how he was making out with tough little Annie. He missed Mickie, especially at night. Without thinking, he'd trail his hand over the side of the bunk to feel for Mickie or listen for the click of claws across the deck as Mickie hunted for a cool spot to sleep. It was the first time they had ever been separated, and he was desperately lonesome for his dog.

Duke was back on the dock, somewhat the worse for the beating Mickie had given him, but once again stalking up and down. Now that Mickie was gone, Duke scarcely noticed Brad.

So the days wore away. The first week of the season was gone.

Then one morning at breakfast Captain Ed said, "How'd you like to see Mickie today?"

"Could we?" Brad asked excitedly.

"We're only a few miles from home. We can cruise that way, as well as any other, looking for salmon. We always stop by to check on Annie after a week or so to make sure she's getting along all right alone."

They pulled in to the little dock late that afternoon. Brad didn't wait to help tie up. He jumped ashore and went racing up the trail and around the corner of the cabin. Mickie was tied to the doghouse. He leaped and barked as he strained at the end of the chain. Brad fell on his knees, wrapped his arms around Mickie's neck, pressed his face against the dog's furry forehead, and crooned: "Mickie! Mickie! I'm so glad to see you. I'm so glad!" Mickie showed his teeth in a grin and licked Brad's face.

Annie came to the door and said, "I figured it was about time you fellows showed up."

As Captain Ed and George came around the corner, George asked: "How about a home-cooked meal, Annie? I'm getting awful tired of my cooking."

"You came all this way for a meal?" Annie grinned.

"That's right."

"Then let's get started. Come on, Brad. You can see your dog after you eat."

The kitchen was stifling with the heat of the day and the stove. The aroma of cooking jam was heavy. Annie shoved a kettle on the back of the stove and got out a pair of frying pans.

It didn't take her long to whip up a meal. While they ate,

she filled them in on her days. "Berries are awful scattery this year and they're little bitty things. I have to scramble to get a gallon. It'll take three, maybe four more days before I'm through. And I'm not sure I won't run outa wood. That punky stuff we cut last fall burns like paper and don't hold the heat. But I'll make out. Now, how's seining?"

"Not good," George said.

"We've been straining water through the seine for almost a week," Captain Ed said. "We're not making the gas bill. The run's stopped dead. I haven't seen it this bad in years."

"I was afraid of something like that. There's hardly any spawners in the creek." Annie figured rapidly, "There's twenty-four days left. They'd better hit soon or we're in trouble."

"Us and every cannery, seiner, and fisherman on the Sound," Captain Ed said.

"It's us I'm worried about."

"We've got to figure it'll hit again," George said. "We've got to keep looking and hoping. I say they'll come"—he glanced at Captain Ed—"and in time to do us some good."

Brad had been sitting eating quietly, saying nothing. But since he'd seen Mickie again, a wild idea was forming. He wanted to be with Mickie, if even for a short time. Now, as he listened to the talk, his idea took the form he felt would appeal. During a lull he said: "As long as the fish aren't running, you don't need me. Why can't I stay with Annie a few days? She can use some help picking berries, now that they're so scarce. And I could cut some extra wood. You'll have to come back this way to go to the cannery with a load of fish if they start running. You could pick us up then."

Captain Ed looked at George. "With the few salmon we're getting we can manage easy," the latter said.

"All right," Captain Ed agreed, "that's not a bad idea. I don't like the idea of Annie running out of wood and having to cut it. It'll also give you and Mickie a couple of days to run around together." He smiled. "But don't look for us to be back for five or six days unless the run hits again and we need you." He shoved back his chair. "Well, we'd better get moving."

Brad, Annie, and Mickie went down to the dock and saw them off. When they returned to the cabin, Annie said: "It's too late to go for more berries today. I'll finish that batch I was working on, and we'll get an early start in the morning." She grinned at Brad. "Sure good to have you back. I was getting kinda lonesome."

When Brad crawled into the cot that night, he was surprised to find he missed the bunk aboard the boat, the sight of Captain Ed and George across the narrow aisle. He missed the cool night air funneling through the port above his head and the gentle lift and fall of the *Annie B.* And, strangely, he missed the knowledge that the sea was just two inches away, beyond the planking.

They were up early, had breakfast, and armed with a bucket each, headed up the slope toward the valley. Annie took the big shotgun. "I never see anything to shoot in summer," she grinned. "I just always feel like I've left something important behind if I don't have a gun."

Mickie led the way, cruising back and forth ahead and behind them, inspecting every clump and brush patch. They entered the valley, following the line they'd taken during the winter, and so came to the brush-choked ravine. Annie said: "There's a patch of berries in a cleared spot in the middle of that ravine. It's the only cleared spot in there. The grass is about a foot high, so you'll have to get on your hands and knees and hunt for 'em. Straight up the valley about a quarter mile is another patch. You take the ravine. I'll go up the valley. I'll hunt you up when I've got a bucketful."

Brad found the patch easily enough. The berries were scattered and small, and the deep grass made picking slow.

Mickie ranged about, exploring through the nearby grass and brush. Finally he chased a parka squirrel down a hole and spent a busy half hour trying to dig it out. He gave up when the permafrost became too hard, and stretched out to rest in the shade of a bush.

The day gradually turned hot. Not a breath of air stirred in the ravine. Filling the bucket was a terribly slow process. Brad became thirsty, and his back ached from the constant stooped position. This was harder than seining. He wondered how thin little Annie did it year after year. The bucket was about half full when he stopped to straighten his aching back and look around. It was quiet. Not even a jay disturbed the silence. Mickie was asleep under the bush. Brad said: "Eat and sleep in the shade. That's a bad life for a dog?"

That moment the shot tore into the silence. On the heels of it came a scream, high, sharp, and filled with agony. Brad was on his feet and running at top speed. That had been the twelve-gauge. The scream was not the deep, gravelly voice he knew so well. But it was Annie's, and she was in terrible trouble.

As fast as Brad was, Mickie was before him. At the first

sound of Annie's scream he was up and away, streaking through the long grass, a gray-white shadow running low to the ground like a wolf, with a wolf's tremendous speed. Brad had barely gained his full stride when Mickie dived into a tangle of brush, and disappeared. He was taking the most direct route to Annie's voice.

Brad knew he'd never make time fighting through the brush, so he circled around it. As he ran he listened for another shot or the sound of Annie's voice again. There was nothing. He tried to imagine what had happened, but could not. Then the fierce exertion of running claimed all his mind. He was tiring. It seemed much farther than he'd thought. His lungs felt as though they'd burst. A ball of pain settled in his chest, spread across his shoulders and into his arms. His legs began to ache, but still he ran.

He burst out of the ravine onto the valley floor, and there were Annie and Mickie before him. The shotgun lay some feet away. The berries had been spilled, the pail smashed flat. Annie sat on the ground, the right sleeve of her shirt ripped away. Her arm was streaming blood from ugly, open wounds. She had both arms locked tight around Mickie's neck as if she'd never let go, and was sobbing, "Mickie! Mickie! Mickie!" Mickie was happily licking the tears from her cheeks.

She looked up at Brad and said in a shaky voice: "Old Toughy jumped me. Mickie saved my life."

"Don't talk," Brad warned. "Sit still." He looked at the wounds on her shoulder and arm. The sight of so much blood frightened him. He had to stop the bleeding. Cold water would help. He caught up the smashed bucket, pulled

138

out the sides as best he could, and ran to the creek and filled it. When he returned he pulled off his shirt and tore it into strips. He soaked the strips in the ice-cold water and held them to the wounds. Gradually the bleeding stopped. When he thought he dared, he wound the strips tight about the wounds, and asked, "Do you think you can walk back to the cabin?"

Annie nodded. A little color was coming back into her pinched cheeks. "He didn't chew on my legs. Help me up." On her feet she would have fallen, but Brad held her up.

"Can you make it?" he asked anxiously. "We've got to get home."

"I'll make it. But you'll have to help me. Let's go." So they began the long, tortuous walk back down the valley, stopping often to rest. Brad carried the shotgun in one hand and steadied Annie with the other. Mickie led the way with a very protective air.

When they finally made the cabin, Annie's face was white and beads of perspiration stood out on her forehead. She sank wearily into a chair at the kitchen table and sat, head down, sick with shock, holding her injured arm tight to her side. She took no interest as Brad got the fire going, heated water, and tore an old sheet into strips for bandages.

Mickie sat on his tail beside her, cocked his head, and watched Brad hurrying about. He had walked into the kitchen as if he belonged, and Brad was too busy to chase him out.

When the water was hot, Brad unwrapped the blood-soaked bandages and cleansed and sterilized the wounds. Annie kept her head turned away while he worked. The arm

139

was not so bad as Brad had at first feared. The point of her shoulder had a bad gash from a claw, he guessed, as Old Toughy struck and knocked her down. That had caused most of the bleeding. Her upper arm bore the clear pattern of the bear's teeth, but the punctures were smooth and the flesh had not been torn. Her arm was not broken. "It's not so bad," he said. "It's going to be all right."

"You sure?" she asked in a small voice.

"I'm sure. Look at it, Annie. Come on, see for yourself."

Annie turned her head fearfully and looked at her arm, then at her shoulder. "Oh, Lord!" she whispered, "I thought I'd be crippled."

"You won't. You can see."

"Yes," she said. "Yes."

The knowledge helped her. By the time Brad had bandaged her arm and fashioned a sling from a towel, most of the color had returned to her cheeks. "You lie down," he said. "I'll take care of everything."

Annie walked into the bedroom alone and lay down, and Brad spread a blanket over her. She managed a smile and said, "Don't know what I'd do without you—you and Mickie."

Mickie came in, went to the head of the bed and thrust his nose up at Annie, and sniffed. Brad started to run him out, but Annie said, "Let him be. But for him I'd be dead." Brad sensed she wanted to talk about it, and let her. "Should have figured Old Toughy'd come back into the valley to eat grass and roots and berries, now that there's no salmon. But I didn't. I'd forgot about him because he's always been up at that special hangout of his up the creek. I heard a noise, and there he was coming right at me."

140

"Did you hit him with that one shot?"

Annie shook her head. "He was on top of me. It went wild. He was draggin' me around, and I was playing dead when Mickie came. He piled into that bear and chewed on him until he let go of me and chased Mickie, who led him away from me. When he couldn't catch the dog, he got discouraged, I guess, and wandered off. He'd forgot about me."

She patted Mickie, who waved his tail and showed his teeth in a grin. "I been awful mean to you," Annie confessed. "I didn't mean it. I didn't want to break my heart when you got old and sick and died. I went through that five times. Why couldn't you be a mean, ugly mutt like Duke?" Her voice broke. She put a hand over her eyes and murmured resignedly: "No use fighting it any longer. Here I go again."

"You rest now," Brad said.

"All right. But you let Mickie stay."

"He's staying." Brad watched Mickie stretch out on the floor at the head of the bed with a contented sigh. Then he went out and softly closed the door.

Brad took the twelve-gauge shotgun, tiptoed outside, and headed up the valley. His bucket half full of strawberries was up there, and maybe he could salvage some of Annie's spilled ones. Because berries were so scarce, they needed them.

He found his own bucket, salvaged much of Annie's, and returned two hours later with a pail almost full. He'd seen no sign of Old Toughy.

He made lunch, but Annie could not eat. Her cheeks were flushed, and she admitted the pain was bad. He gave her

141

two pain pills from a bottle on the shelf, and after an hour she said they'd helped. Then, at her directions, he cleaned the strawberries, put them in a kettle, and made the jam. He washed jars and filled them, and when they'd cooled, carried them to the freeze room. By the time he'd finished, the sun was swinging down the western sky, heading for its bed in the sea, and it was time to get supper.

Annie insisted she was not hungry, but he made a broth from a chunk of venison and prevailed upon her to taste it. She ended by drinking a full cup. Afterward she said: "I can't pick berries for a couple of weeks. By then they'll be gone. What'll you fellows do for jam and fresh frozen strawberries this winter?"

"Don't worry about it," Brad said. "We'll talk it over in the morning. You try and get some sleep."

She looked at him, her usually sharp blue eyes dulled with pain. "You figuring to do it alone? It's too dangerous with Old Toughy up there. You hear?"

"I know," Brad said. "You want another pain pill?"

"Yes, and open the window. It's hot in here."

It wasn't hot. She had a fever. But he opened the window and brought her another pill. "You fed Mickie?" she asked.

"Going to do that now."

He fed Mickie, and the dog returned to the bedroom and curled up in the same spot near the head of the bed. Brad closed the door and returned to the kitchen. He sat thinking of Annie's injury and of tomorrow. She wanted more berries, and they needed them for the coming winter. He could pick the berries, but he didn't like the thought of Old Toughy being around. He could probably avoid him. But Annie would be up and around in a few days, and she'd be going into the valley later to pick blueberries and blackberries. Old Toughy would be a menace to her all season. And by the look of her arm and shoulder, he guessed, she wouldn't handle a gun for some time, at least not the big rifle. Where was she going to get protection after he went back seining?

He was looking idly up at the gunrack and the big rifle, when a thought drifted into his mind. It so startled him that he immediately rejected it. But the thought refused to go away. Then he realized that his own thinking had been taking him in that direction. It's logical, he told himself. There's no harm thinking about it. It's a job that needs doing. Annie can't, and Captain Ed and George won't be back for days. Even then, they haven't the time to do it.

He could do it. He'd become good with the little twenty-gauge shotgun, and he'd fired the light rifle that time at the running wolves. The shot hadn't carried because the rifle was too small, but he'd been dead in line with the wolf. Handling the big rifle would be no different. It was just a lot more gun, and that's what this job took. He could leave before Annie was awake to stop him. And he'd take Mickie. He couldn't do it without Mickie. He'd hunt with the utmost care, keeping his eyes and ears open. He'd take no chances.

Brad didn't know just when he passed the point of thinking about it and realized he was committed to the act. The sun plunged into the sea, and the night shadows lay deep across the yard. Far up the shadowed slope the mouth of the valley took on a dark and mysterious look. Inside, the kitchen lay in deepest gloom, but the boy paid no attention. He was carefully, methodically planning the death of Old Toughy.

nine

Brad was up early. He wanted to be gone before Annie was awake. He tiptoed across the kitchen, stealthily opened her door, and peeked in. She was asleep, and it seemed to be a restful sleep. She needed it. It had been a rough night. He'd been up twice: once to get her a drink, the second time to give her more pain pills. The last two seemed to have quieted her down. The angry flush was gone from her cheeks. Her color looked almost normal. He guessed the fever was leaving.

Mickie still lay on the floor at the head of the bed. Sometime during the night Annie had dropped Captain Ed's pillow on the floor for him, and now he lay stretched full length, his big head on the pillow, watching Brad. His tail thumped the floor in recognition, and Brad made motions for him to come. Mickie rose and clicked across the floor into the kitchen. Brad carefully closed the door.

He'd like to eat before he left. He'd be plenty hungry before he got back. But any extra noise might wake Annie.

He placed a chair under the gunrack, stepped on the seat, and looked at the big rifle. All winter he'd studied the gun day after day, and the temptation to take it down, to handle it, had been almost overwhelming. Now he was going to, and suddenly he was afraid to touch it. After a little, he reached up and lifted it down. Then he just stood there holding it in his hands. It was heavier than he'd expected. It was solid and beautiful and utterly deadly. He ran a hand down the gleaming barrel and along the polished stock. Now, with the full weight of it in his hands, the realization of what he meant to do came home to him with shocking force. He remembered Old Toughy charging Mickie this spring, hair up, every tooth gleaming, the full-throated roar of rage that had fairly shaken the earth and frozen him in his tracks. Old Toughy would be coming at him that way if he got the chance. A cold ball of fear settled in his stomach, and last night's brave resolve began leaking away. The temptation to put the big rifle back in the rack was as great as his desire to take it down had ever been. He spent a bad minute fighting his fear back in place.

He was a good shot and he had a gun powerful enough to drop the biggest animal. And he had Mickie. Mickie had saved Annie, and earlier this spring he had actually attacked the bear. He could count on Mickie to smell or hear Toughy and warn him. They could do it. He stepped down from the chair. With that single act all doubt and uncertainty vanished. He was committed to hunting down and killing Old Toughy.

He filled his pockets with shells from the table drawer and, with Mickie at his heels, tiptoed outside and closed the door.

He stepped into a gray, chill morning. During the night fog had drifted in from the sea, and now it hung over the land in sleazy, motionless banners and columns that blotted out the valley's mouth, the snow-capped mountains beyond, and hid the early-morning sun. Looking toward the sea, Brad barely made out the line of the beach less than two hundred feet away.

The fog would give Old Toughy an advantage. He wouldn't be able to spot the bear and shoot from a long, safe distance as he'd planned. He'd be on top of Old Toughy now before he knew it. But there was no breeze. That took part of the advantage from the bear. His keen nose couldn't pick up their scent a mile or so away and warn him. In time the warming sun would burn the fog off. But Brad couldn't wait, because Annie was sure to wake before then. He'd have to go ahead, be especially careful and quiet, and ready every second. "Keep Mickie close," he warned himself.

Brad waited until they were several hundred yards from the cabin before he loaded the rifle and jacked a shell into the barrel.

Mickie wanted to range far and wide, but Brad kept calling him back. "You stay with me," he cautioned. "I might need you bad in a hurry. Don't go running off out of sight. Stay close, Mickie. Stay. Stay." Mickie finally seemed to understand, and ranged only a few feet on either side.

They were into the valley before Brad realized it, and the fog was thicker than ever. The mountains and the steep valley sides had trapped it. Without a chance to drift, it had packed in thick. It clung in sparkling drops to the long grass-blades, and soon he was soaked to the knees. It dripped from the outer edges of leaves and put a glass-slick sheen on the face of rocks, tree trunks, and limbs. Soon Mickie's coat was plastered to his body, as if he'd been in a driving rain. The sounds of all bird and animal life were stilled. There was a feeling of eerie unreality in this sleazy, silent world.

Brad came to the spot where the bear had jumped Annie, and stopped. From here he wasn't sure which way to go. Old Toughy could be anywhere. He could be lying up in a brush patch or he might be out on the open valley floor eating grass or digging up roots and bulbs. He might even be down at the creek looking for salmon. Brad wished that the sun would break through and burn the fog away or that a breeze would stir it around. "No, no wind," he told himself. That would carry his scent to Old Toughy, and he didn't want that. He'd stay in the open, he decided, and skirt around the patches of brush. From here on, he could expect to run into the bear any second.

He was glad that he'd hunted the valley all winter with Annie and that he'd tramped over it this spring; otherwise he'd be hopelessly lost. Now he carried a picture of the valley in his mind. He recognized every brush patch and cleared spot as it came out of the fog, and knew exactly where he was and what manner of terrain he could expect next. In this way he and Mickie moved slowly, almost silently up the valley. Mickie sensed the boy's caution and nervousness, and stayed close.

The sun peeked through once, then was lost again. A vagrant breeze stirred the fog.

After they had continued for almost an hour, Brad knew the valley was narrowing down, preparing to squeeze between the mountains. Toughy would not hang out on the valley floor because the things he liked to eat were running

147

out. Here he'd be checking the creek for salmon. There was a good spot nearby where the water was shallow and the bank sandy. Brad turned toward the creek.

He knew he was nearing the creek when the silence was broken by the sharp cry of a fishing eagle. On the heels of that sound a crow set up a noisy racket in the nearby brush, then was silent. The crow started up again, and kept talking in an angry, inquisitive voice. The crow's voice meant nothing to Brad until Mickie stopped, head down, tail stretched straight out, his whole body tense. At that instant the crow's voice stopped, and he flapped briefly into sight through the fog.

Brad moved quickly to a rotting stump, slid the rifle over the top, and stood perfectly still, his heart hammering. He caught a whisper of sound, like that of brush scraping softly against a passing body. He saw a bush move, glimpsed brown fur against the green of fog-wet leaves. Then the bear was in full view, rolling out of the fog straight toward Brad like something from another world. Old Toughy looked bigger, heavier, and much sleeker than he had this spring. His limp was hardly noticeable. His great head was down and he was sniffing along the ground, unconscious of the boy less than a hundred feet away. His huge shoulders rolled at each stride. Ropes of muscles bunched and crawled beneath his loose-fitting hide.

Brad eased the gun forward and dropped his cheek against

Brad eased the gun forward and dropped his cheek against the smooth, cold stock.

148

the smooth, cold stock. At that moment the bear turned sharply and headed for the creek. In a couple of seconds he'd be lost in the fog. Brad searched frantically for the shoulder with the cross hairs, found it, and squeezed the trigger.

He was not prepared for the thunderous explosion. A hammer blow smashed into his shoulder with such force it almost jolted the rifle from his hands. He worked the bolt frantically, jacking in a fresh shell. The bear whirled with a snarl and bit at the spot the bullet had struck. Then Mickie charged, bellowing in full voice. The next instant bear and dog vanished in the fog.

Brad listened to their crashing progress toward the creek. Only when he heard the unmistakable splashing of water did he think to call Mickie back. He tried to whistle, but his mouth and lips were dry. When he put two fingers in his mouth to try to whistle, he realized his hands were shaking. It was the third try before he brought forth a shrill, far-reaching sound.

His ears kept ringing, and his shoulder ached from the kick of the shot. He'd forgotten Annie's first rule: hold the stock tight to the shoulder. All he had to do to handle the big rifle, he knew now, was remember the rules Annie had drilled into him for killing ptarmigans with the little twenty-gauge.

He hadn't stopped Old Toughy, but that bullet had gone where he'd aimed because the bear had bit at the very spot. He whistled again for Mickie, and a minute later the dog appeared out of the fog, tongue hanging out, panting. Brad patted him and said, "You did fine."

Mickie was wet, but only with dew. The sounds of splashing had been Old Toughy crossing the creek on a run. He hadn't charged, Brad thought, and that was strange. Or maybe he had. The fog had bounced the noise of the shot around so, it had misplaced the direction of sound. Toughy had been heading for the creek, and he'd charged straight ahead.

Brad's first thought was to follow immediately. But he knew better. If you crippled a brownie, wait, let the shot stiffen up his muscles and make him sick. The danger was in going after him immediately when he might be lying up someplace waiting to jump you.

He'd heard Toughy hit the creek, so it was safe to go that far. They stopped a few feet short, and Brad knew it was the sandy, shallow spot where the bear liked to fish. He sat down to wait. Mickie lay beside him, but his head was up, his sharp ears pricked forward as he watched and listened.

Brad had no idea how long he waited, but his shoulder had stopped aching and his ears no longer rang. Twice the sun broke through. Finally it stayed. Its heat began to melt the fog, and slowly the valley emerged. A breeze sprang up and blew the last streamers away, and the valley lay bright and sunny. Brad could see the snow-crested mountains again. The grass dried, and the leaves no longer shone with a film of water. The eagle returned, lighted on a snag, and sat with wings spread, searching the creek for salmon with cold, sharp eyes. Finally, disappointed, he sprang into the air and let the currents ferry him toward the distant sea. A flock of crows went over, talking among themselves. A jay began chattering in the thicket.

The sun was getting high, and Brad guessed he'd waited

long enough. Old Toughy must be pretty sick by now, and beginning to stiffen up. Brad stood up, and Mickie rose with him. He checked the rifle and fiddled with the bolt. There was a great hollow in the pit of his stomach. Even with Old Toughy hard hit, this next encounter could be terribly dangerous. The bear was alerted now, and angry. He dreaded their meeting more than anything he had ever faced. But it had to be done. "Let's go," he said in a hoarse whisper to Mickie, and together they moved toward the creek.

In the soft sand of the creek bank Brad found Old Toughy's prints leading into the water. The opposite bank was higher. He made out the top of a brush patch that set back some distance from the creek. He bet Old Toughy was holed up in there. Maybe by now he was dead. But he had to make sure.

Mickie trotted to the water's edge, smelled the tracks, and looked back at Brad. "Go ahead." Brad motioned him across the stream. "I'll be right behind you. Go on."

The stream was only a foot deep and some forty feet wide. Mickie plunged in and went lunging across. Brad followed. The bottom was rocky, and he had to watch his step for fear of falling. He had progressed less than a third of the way when Mickie growled, then began to bark frantically. Brad looked up, and there, lunging down the bank, every tooth shining, charged Old Toughy.

Mickie's hundred pounds piled straight into him as he reached for a hold on the bear's tender nose. Old Toughy swing a lightning-swift paw and sent Mickie rolling end over end ten feet away.

Brad had the rifle up and his cheek snuggled against the

stock. The long, slim barrel came down, and the cross hairs centered on Old Toughy's broad head. It was like shooting ptarmigans; only, Toughy was slower and his head much larger. Brad pressed the trigger as the bear hit the creek in a shower of spray. He worked the bolt swiftly, and another shell rose into the firing chamber. But it wasn't needed. Old Toughy took one long lunging stride into the water; then all that marvelous strength deserted him and he collapsed with a great splash, and was still.

Brad held the gun on him, waiting. Then he realized that Old Toughy was dead, because his head was partially underwater and he didn't raise it to breathe. Brad waded forward cautiously, holding the rifle ready. He punched the bear's side with the muzzle but got no response. He turned and waded back to shore. He began to tremble, and his legs were weak. He sat down on the sand and waited for the feeling to pass. He drew a deep breath and let it out in a long sigh. He felt as if he'd just wakened from a nightmare.

Mickie waded slowly across the stream, favoring a front leg. Brad inspected it, feeling for broken bones. There were none. Old Toughy's blow had grazed the dog's shoulder, and, Brad guessed, bruised his muscles. "You darned fool," he said, and held Mickie close. "You didn't have to jump on him. I was ready. If he'd hit you in the ribs, he'd have caved in every one and you'd be dead." Mickie grinned, and licked the boy's face.

Brad picked up the rifle, rose, and stood looking at the big body half submerged in the stream. A tremendous elation surged through him, and he felt strong and sure of himself. He'd handled the big rifle. He'd met the biggest, most dangerous animal in North America and he'd killed it cleanly. Then he thought of the years Old Toughy had lived in this valley. He thought of him digging roots, rolling rocks, ripping stumps apart with his massive strength, catching salmon from the stream, and roaring and raging and scaring every living creature for miles around. A part of this wonderful valley Brad loved so much was gone. It would never again be quite the same. He felt sad that he had had to kill the animal. He said to Mickie, "Let's go home," and turned away, with Mickie limping painfully beside him. Brad didn't look back. But he knew he'd never forget the picture of Old Toughy lying in the stream, the swift water boiling around his big body as if it had been there forever.

Annie was on the back porch leaning against a post, waiting for them. She looked haggard and her face was drawn. Her thin body seemed smaller than ever. For the first time she looked almost fragile. "I heard the shot," she said, and the rough quality was gone from her voice. "I'd have come up there but I knew I couldn't make it. Besides, with this bum arm I'd have been in the way. So I waited. It was a mighty long wait."

"How's your arm feel?"

"Stiff. But the pain's gone."

"I wanted to get back before you woke up. I knew you'd be worried. But I couldn't. Old Toughy's dead," he said, but found no pleasure in telling her. Now that the excitement and tension of the hunt were over, he felt let down, depressed.

"I figured that. I see you're all right."

"I'm fine."

155

Mickie limped up to Annie, waving his tail, and lifted his nose to sniff at her. She rubbed his ears and tried to smile, but it didn't quite come off.

"He charged Toughy," Brad said, "and got knocked flying. But there's no broken bones."

Annie continued to rub Mickie's ears. She couldn't look at Brad. "That's a good way to get killed," she said to Mickie.

"He thought he was protecting me." Brad went into the kitchen and leaned the rifle in a corner.

Annie followed and lowered herself carefully into a chair. Mickie came in and sat on his tail beside her. Annie said, "You could have been killed, too. Why didn't you tell me what you planned to do?"

"I wasn't killed. And if I'd told you, you'd have yelled that Old Toughy was too big for me to tackle, that the rifle was too much gun for me to handle. You'd have been upset, and you needed rest."

"I was plenty upset when I discovered you and the big rifle and Mickie all gone. I knew what you were up to."

"It had to be done."

"But you're a boy. No fifteen-year-old boy goes hunting rogue brownies." Some of the gravel was coming back into Annie's voice.

"I did. And it's over. As soon as we have breakfast I'm going after more berries. I'm going to pick berries up in the valley for a couple of days and I can't be looking out for Old Toughy. After I go fishing, you'll be up there picking blackberries and blueberries, and you can't be looking out, either. Besides, you won't be able to handle a gun for some time. I didn't want to kill him. I had to."

"You scared the living daylights out of me. Don't you ever

156

do that again." Her small face was all puckered up, and Brad thought tough little Stampede Annie was going to cry. She looked down quickly and rubbed Mickie's ears.

"I won't. Toughy's dead." As Brad glanced about the kitchen, he noticed that the stove was cold. "You haven't had anything to eat, have you?"

"I couldn't eat."

"How about now?" He grinned at her. "I could eat the hide off a skunk. We've got fresh blueberries in the freeze room, and I could make you some toast and beat up some eggs and chop up some bacon and make an omelet."

"Sounds good. Maybe I could eat a little." She watched Brad lay the kindling and get the fire going before she said thoughtfully, "I suppose you'll take the big rifle when you go after berries?"

"Yes," he said. "But I don't expect to use it. I didn't see any other brownies or any sign."

"You'll be careful?"

"I'll be careful."

Annie watched Brad get out the bacon, cut two slices, dice them, and put them in a frying pan. He broke four eggs in a bowl and beat them. He did it just the way she would have done it. While the frying pan was getting hot, he ran out to the freeze room and returned with a can of blueberries. He emptied them into two bowls, sugared them, and put them on the table. The bacon was sizzling, and he pured in the egg batter and the satisfying aroma drifted through the room.

Mickie's black nose began to twitch and he licked his lips. Annie said, "Don't worry; you'll get your share."

When they finally sat down at the table, Annie was smiling and some of her cheerfulness had returned. "Can't

157

remember when anybody else cooked a meal for me and I just watched. Sure smells good. I guess I am hungry. You're getting right handy around the kitchen, too."

"I watched you all winter and spring." They smiled at each other and began to eat in companionable silence.

After they had finished and Annie sat sipping her coffee, Brad put what was left in a pan for Mickie, added chunks of bread, poured hot bacon grease over it, and put it on the floor.

He started to pick up the dishes, but Annie said: "You go on. I can do this and wash dishes one-handed."

"You want me to look at your arm before I go?"

"No, it feels good. Let's let well enough alone till tonight."

Brad went for the big rifle. "I'll be back in time to fix lunch. You rest."

"I will." Annie watched him handle the rifle with the same sure ease he had handled the little twenty-gauge. "You got enough shells?"

He felt in his pockets. "I've got three."

"Take three or four more." As she watched him get the shells, she was about to caution him to be careful; then she bit back the words and said nothing.

Mickie finished his meal and started to limp after Brad.

"Maybe you'd like him to stay for company."

Annie looked at Mickie waiting expectantly, and shook her head. "He thinks it's part of his job to go along and take care of you. I agree. Nothing can sneak up on Mickie. I'll feel better if he's with you."

"All right," Brad said. "Let's go."

Annie watched them go out into the bright sunlight and start up the slope toward the mouth of the valley. He knew he could handle that rifle, she thought. Why didn't I?

ten

For the next two days Brad and Mickie spent all their mornings up in the valley. Brad would lean the rifle against a stump or log and then crawl about on hands and knees through the thick grass, gathering the small strawberries. Mickie would lie down beside the rifle, head up, ears pricked forward, eyes roving over the valley floor. He seemed to know his job was to be on guard, and not even a mouse running through the nearby grass escaped his sharp attention.

On the second afternoon Brad finished making the jam. Annie stood in the doorway of the freeze room, surveyed the rows of full jars, and announced happily: "That's as fine a batch as I've ever seen. We've go plenty now. You can quit."

"I finished just in time, then," Brad said. "We're almost out of wood. Tomorrow I'll have to cut more."

The next morning Brad chose a tree near the beach, felled it, and began cutting it into blocks with the crosscut saw. It was slow, hard work. He had less than a quarter of it cut when the mail boat poked into view late that afternoon. Brad ran down to the dock and jumped aboard.

Captain Bob Masters handed him the mail, and asked, "How do you like living here?"

"Fine," he said. "Did you go by my old home?"

"Yep, and everything seems to be okay."

They talked a minute longer, then Brad left and the *Vixen* churned back to sea. Brad searched through the mail. There were some papers, a catalogue, and a couple of magazines. There was no letter from his aunt. Though he heaved a sigh of relief, he was puzzled. Knowing something about Aunt Clara, he felt sure there should have been an immediate answer to the kind of letter Annie wrote. Then he guessed what might have happened. Almost every summer Aunt Clara took a trip. One year she'd gone to Europe; another time she'd taken a world cruise. Another summer she'd gone to some foreign college for special courses. Maybe she was gone somewhere again. In that case she wouldn't return until school started in the fall. Then it would be too late to do anything about him for another year.

He ran up to the cabin and gave the mail to Annie. She searched through it. "Humph," she snorted. "I figured there'd be a letter from your aunt. She's had plenty of time."

"I told you I didn't mean anything to her."

"So you did. I just don't understand a woman like that."

Brad left Annie shaking her head, and happily returned to cutting wood.

Near the end of the third day of woodcutting he was piling the last of the cut-up tree on the porch when the

Annie B pulled in to the dock and Captain Ed and George strode up the trail.

Brad met them and asked, "Has the run started?"

"Not much," Captain Ed said. "We've about three thousand in the hold now. That's the most we've had since we left. How're things here?" Then he and George saw Annie in the doorway, her arm in a sling. They bore down on her, pouring out a stream of questions.

"All right," Annie said, "come inside and I'll tell you all about it."

Sitting at the kitchen table, Annie launched into the happenings since Brad returned. Mickie came in and sat down beside her. She patted him, and George and Captain Ed looked at each other but said nothing. "If it wasn't for Mickie," Annie said, "I'd be long dead."

Brad listened, as fascinated as Captain Ed and George, as Annie told how Old Toughy had attacked her, how she'd been saved by Mickie, and how Mickie and he had hunted down and killed the big bear. "Hunted him up there in the valley in the fog! In fog so thick you could cut it with a knife, mind you. Used the big rifle like he'd been born to it. Got Toughy back of the shoulder with the first shot. Then waited for the fog to lift and the bear to get sick, and went after him again. Mickie got slapped head over heels. Then Brad killed him with one shot right between the eyes, with Old Toughy charging him, too. Did it as good as any old-timer could." Brad thought the hunt sounded much more thrilling the way Annie told it.

"And Brad took over the kitchen, picked the berries, and even made the jam. Then he cut and lugged in a whole bunch of wood. I been well taken care of. Fact is, things couldn't be better than if I hadn't got hurt," Annie said proudly.

George thumbed back his old hat, and grinned. "Compared to here, not much. Eh, Skipper?"

"That's right. We've just been running the seine through the sea like everybody else. But I've a hunch they're going to hit real soon. We figured to take Brad with us, but not in the shape you're in. We'll try to find a man."

"No you don't! I can make out fine alone now. Blueberries won't begin for a couple of weeks at least. I've got plenty of wood, and I can cook one-handed. You take Brad. Mickie and I'll make out fine."

"You sure?" Captain Ed was skeptical. "Don't try to be tough."

"The arm's feeling good. It's stiff and sore, but that's leaving. You get out and catch those fish. We need 'em."

"All right." Captain Ed leaned forward and rubbed Mickie's head. "I feel a lot better with you here. Take good care of her, Mickie."

Once again the *Annie B* was back at sea with a full crew. They cruised long hours, with Brad and George taking turns spotting. They caught a few. "About enough to pay the gas bill," George said. "Maybe a little more."

Many skippers didn't even go out, figuring there was no use when they barely made expenses. More than a hundred boats lay at the dock in Orca City. Others anchored in small groups of three and four in quiet bays and inlets. The crews played cards, read and slept and talked endlessly about the failure of the run. But many others still combed the sea day after day, searching, hoping. They returned with their meager catches, gassed up, and headed out to sea again, doggedly determined not to quit. The *Annie B* was one of them.

But one hopeless day was like the next. Captain Ed's hunch that the run would hit was forgotten. There came a day when George no longer voiced his hope. Slowly the season drew toward the closing date, and there was no change. Finally Captain Ed and George both admitted the inevitable.

They anchored in a quiet cove to catch some sleep. They'd finished supper and were sitting at the table in the darkened galley just before turning in. The night was warm and breathless; the sea was without a ripple. Silence was a cloak thrown loosely over the earth, broken only by the murmur of night life along the beach. Captain Ed said in a tired voice: "Three days of season left. Did you realize that? Even if the run hit now, it wouldn't do us any good."

"Why? We can catch a lot of salmon in three days," Brad said.

"We can catch 'em, but we can't deliver 'em to the cannery fast enough," Captain Ed said. "Every time you get a load, you've got to take it in. That's what eats up time."

George stretched his long legs, and scowled. "We're going down fighting, aren't we?"

"Of course. But we'll go down. In all my twenty-five years' seining I've never seen a year like this. The Bureau of Fisheries really missed their forecast this time."

"I've never known them to miss this far," George said. "I don't see how they could, but they did."

Next to the last day they gathered in a small school of several thousand and ran in to the cannery with them. "This could be our last load," Captain Ed said darkly.

"Could be." George scowled at the flat sea. "Wonder if it'd do any good to talk to Karlson. He might have one charitable bone in his system."

"Why should he? Look what he's getting for a measly fifteen thousand. But we'll talk to him. I'll try anything."

Today there were more boats than ever tied to the dock and along the float. Brad guessed they were waiting the end of the season, a day away. As the *Annie B* pulled under the conveyor and they were getting the hatches off, the fish counter called down, "Hey! you heard the news?"

"What news?" George asked.

"The Bureau of Fisheries has extended the season two weeks."

"Good!" George shouted, "Good!"

"What does that mean?" Brad asked.

"We've got two more weeks to look for fish," Captain Ed explained. "It means the Bureau hasn't given up on their prediction of a big run."

"That'll help, won't it?"

"It will if the run comes." Captain Ed put an arm around Brad's shoulders, and some of his black mood fell away, "Anyway, it's two more weeks of grace. We'll use it all."

"Why don't these other skippers go out?"

"They probably figure: So the season's been extended, but

In the following days it seemed that the seiners lying at the dock were right. There were no more salmon.

nothing's changed. There's still no run and maybe won't be. There's no sense wasting gas and wearing out your motor until there's fish. Maybe they're smart. But it's not my way."

In the following days it seemed that the seiners lying at the dock were right. There were no more salmon. Extending the season hadn't helped. On the evening of the third day the *Annie B* came in with a small load. They had just finished unloading when a bald, lean old seiner came down the float and stepped aboard. He was Andy Baxter, a friend of Captain Ed and George.

They all crowded into the galley. Over a steaming cup of coffee Baxter said: "I heard something this afternoon, and again tonight. I'm going to tell you fellows because we've always been good friends. You can make up your own minds about it. I talked with Ted Jensen this afternoon, and he's heading for the far upper end of the Sound. His brother Harry is up there with another boat. Ted said Harry had called him on shortwave and told him the run had hit up there and hit big."

"Stories like that have been running around all season, Andy," Captain Ed said.

"I know it. But hear this. . . . This evening I turned on the shortwave and picked up the Sandy Point Trap. The watchmen were reporting in to the cannery in code."

"They're supposed to," George said, "so the fish pirates won't guess they've got a load they can steal."

"Exactly!" Baxter said triumphantly. "I've been picking up their broadcast all season, and they've been reporting to the cannery in English because they had nothing in the trap. Now suddenly it's in code. See what I mean?"

Captain Ed rubbed his long jaw thoughtfully but said nothing.

"That's not all," Baxter continued. "Shelter Bay Trap has been reporting to the cannery the same way, just 'No fish. No fish.' Tonight they're in code, too. Those two traps are just a mile apart at the far upper end of the Sound." Andy Baxter finished his coffee and stood up. "So maybe it's nothing and I'm grabbing at straws. But it can't be any worse than this end of the Sound. I'm giving it a try."

After Baxter had gone, George asked, "What do you think?"

"You always hear these rumors when they're not running." Captain Ed rubbed a hand across his face and was thoughtful. "Andy's pretty reliable. What he said makes sense. It could be."

"It's a long run," George pointed out. "If it's true, it's too far to bring the fish back here to Karlson, as our contract calls for. And if it's a false alarm we'll be no worse off than we are now. It's a last-gasp effort if we go."

Captain Ed nodded. "We could take the fish to Sunny Bay Cannery or Garden Cove. Under this year's circumstances, what else can a seiner do except to go where the fish are. Let's give it that last try."

An hour later they had refueled and were boring through the quiet night sea toward the far end of the Sound. Captain Ed and George were in the wheelhouse. They would take turns at the wheel and run all night so they could reach their destination some time the next morning. Brad turned in. He lay in his bunk staring at the ceiling till the steady throb of the motor lulled him to sleep.

He awoke to the aroma of fried eggs, bacon, and hot coffee. It took but a minute to dress, and when he entered the galley George had breakfast on the table. Captain Ed was at the wheel. The *Annie B* was still boring steadily through the sea.

"You and I'll eat," George explained. "Then I'll take the wheel while Skipper eats. You can climb up and start spotting after you eat. We're not far from where Andy Baxter said they were running."

An hour later they spotted jumpers and ran out the seine. When they gathered it in they had about a thousand. Captain Ed said, "So far we're no better off than before."

They began cruising across the sea again. Another hour passed, and another. The sun climbed high in the sky. The day turned hot. They saw boats in the distance, but so far away they couldn't tell if they were loaded. Noon came, and Captain Ed called up: "I'm heading for the Sunny Bay Cannery to get rid of these. Maybe they'll know something, but I'm beginning to get the feeling we've drawn a blank here, too."

The Sunny Bay Cannery was a cluster of white toy buildings against a green mountain background when, without warning, they were in the middle of the biggest school Brad had ever seen. Salmon were flashing silvery in the sunlight for hundreds of yards all around them.

Brad cried at the top of his lungs, "Fish! Fish! Salmon!" He almost fell overboard in his anxiety to get down. As fast as he was, Captain Ed had already stopped the *Annie B* and

169

George had tumbled into the skiff and started the outboard motor with a roar. The nine-hundred-foot seine streamed off the turntable into the sea.

They could not circle even a third of the school, and when they finally worked the pocket close and looked inside it was a mass of churning, twisting silver the like of which Brad had never seen. George looked up, his big, scarred face shining. "Andy was right! Oh, by golly, Andy was right!"

"Right as rain." Captain Ed's laugh was a sudden explosion of the tension that had been building for days.

This, Brad thought, was what they'd been waiting for. This was what he'd strained his eyes until they ached for. For this a thousand boats and thousands of people had come north to work. Many hoped to earn their year's wages during the salmon run, which was the lifeblood of Orca City and a dozen other fishing villages along the coast. Here was more than just gold. Here was food. Food for people, for the brown bears who'd waited so patiently; for the foxes, eagles, gulls, hawks, and a whole host of small animals and birds that scavengered in the wake of others. Here was the year's wages for the crew of the *Annie B.* Here was security for their boat.

Brad was struck by a frightening thought, and looked at Captain Ed, "Could this be just a lucky school, the only one around?"

Captain Ed's laugh was deep and happy. "Not and be this big. When you've been in this business as long as I have, you'll know the real thing when you see it. You're seeing it. Run out the brail, son. Run it out and stand by for a lot of work. We're going to have salmon coming out of our ears."

170

eleven

Captain Ed was right. The run had hit at this far upper end of the Sound and it had hit big. It looked as if their gamble was going to pay off.

"Champ," George said, and grinned, "you're gonna ache before we're through."

The run held steady. Day after day they were out scooping in salmon. They worked from daylight until long after dark. Day after day they wallowed in to the cannery, the *Annie B's* stern almost awash with the weight of their catch. Each night Brad fell into his bunk, sometimes almost too tired to eat. But each dawn he was ready to go. Captain Ed and George were smiling and happy, and Brad was happier than he'd been in a long time.

The end of the season came. Even the last day worked out to perfection. They spotted a big school, ran out the seine, and then brailed the pocket. As the last brailful swung aboard and was dumped into the already bulging hold, Captain Ed called, "That's it! The season's over."

171

George glanced at his watch, and laughed, "We made it! By golly, we made it almost to the second."

They had wound up the season with seven big loads in the Sunny Bay Cannery and they had the equivalent of two big loads back at Orca City.

George and Brad unloaded their catch at the cannery while Captain Ed went to the office to settle up. They had emptied the holds and were sitting in the galley when Captain Ed returned. He waved the check under their noses, and laughed, "Enough here to pay off Karlson, give you your cut, George, Brad a share, and have some left. And we've still got money coming from Karlson. Not bad for the first year." He patted the *Annie B*'s wheel lovingly, "She's ours now, free and clear. Man! is that a load off my back! Let's get back and settle up with Karlson and go tell Annie. She's going to be crazy to know." He stopped then, and added, "I just heard that two days after we left the lower Sound the run hit there, too."

"As big as here?"

"That's what they say."

"Who'd have thought that would happen? But that's seining."

"That's right," Captain Ed agreed. "But it's odd how it worked out. Well, we're through for the year. Let's go." He started the motor, and the *Annie B* slipped away from the dock and headed into the Sound, pointed toward Orca City.

They arrived late the next afternoon. The dock, the float, and the bay were full of seiners. Brad knew their owners were settling up with the half-dozen canneries in the area and preparing to scatter for home.

The three of them went up the dock to Karlson's office. A crowd of fishermen milled about on the dock, discussing the season just past, swapping stories, and comparing catches.

Duke lay on the floor at Karlson's feet, and he looked as ugly as ever.

Karlson was at the desk behind the railing, and his close-set eyes bored at them. "Where were you when the run hit here?" he demanded in his grating voice.

"The upper end of the Sound," Captain Ed said. "We heard they were running up there, and when we got there, they were. Until yesterday, we didn't know the run had hit down here." He produced the check and extended it toward Karlson, "We're ready to settle up for gas, oil, a couple of shirts, the damage to the store that time—and I'll take the mortagage on the *Annie B.*"

"Not so fast!" Karlson leaned back in his chair and said calmly: "You can put that check away. I'm not interested."

"What do you mean, 'not interested'?"

"That mortgage says fifteen thousand, plus a guarantee to deliver to me all the fish you catch during the season. Well, why didn't you?"

"You know why. We had to go where the fish were running. That happened to be at the far end of the Sound. It was too far to bring them back here. You know that."

"Getting those fish to Orca City Cannery was your problem. Mine is to put up a pack. Every fish you took to another cannery I had a right to expect. I was counting on them."

"You got every one just as long as we were close enough to bring them in. But when we had to go to the upper end of the Sound, we were a hundred miles too far away. As you

173

say," Captain Ed remarked quietly, "your job is to put up a pack. Ours is to pay off the mortgage you hold and to catch fish and bring them to you as long as possible. We did that. Now, we're prepared to pay off that mortgage. As a matter of fact, Frank, you didn't need our fish. You got your pack when they hit down here." Captain Ed leaned over the railing, black eyes boring into Karlson. "You're using a phony excuse to try to steal the *Annie B*. And we both know it."

"I'm living up to the letter of that contract. I expect you to do the same."

Captain Ed shook his head. "That excuse won't wash. What we did has been common practice in the North since canneries began almost a hundred years ago."

"You didn't have to go to the other end of the Sound for fish," Karlson insisted. "They hit here in plenty of time for you to get your catch and bring 'em in."

"We didn't know that when we left. Any seiner would have done the same with our information. There's no sense discussing this any further."

"You're right," Karlson snapped. "You've lost the *Annie B* to me, and that's the simple truth."

"I'll handle this." George surged against the rail, his big hand reaching for Karlson.

"No!" Captain Ed grabbed his arm. "Wait, George."

Duke rose from the floor, his chest rumbling ominously, heavy lips lifted away from the long teeth.

George snatched up a chair, "Make your brute behave or put him outside," he warned. "I'll splatter his brains all over this room."

174

Once again he was not the big, friendly George. Brad thought he looked more menacing than Duke.

Karlson looked at George, and believed him. He said: "Lay down, Duke! Lay down, I said!" Duke sank back to the floor. Karlson turned on Captain Ed then, his round cheeks quivering. "Keep that big gorilla away from me or I'll have the law on you! I'm right, and you know it." He pointed a shaking finger at George. "That big ape ain't bluffing me out this time."

"I never bluff," George growled.

"You've wanted the *Annie B* from the first," Captain Ed said to Karlson. "She'd make you a dandy trap tender, and you need one. According to the letter of our contract you're legally right. But there's more to it than that, and we both know it. Contract or not, what we did has always been understood and accepted. It's the unwritten law in the North."

"This'll hold up in court," Karlson snapped.

"Probably." Captain Ed stood there frowning. In the silence, the noise from the crowd of fishermen on the dock came into the office. Brad saw Captain Ed turn and study the fishermen a thoughtful moment. Then he swung back to Karlson. "There's one court where your contract won't hold up, Frank: the seiners themselves."

"How's that?"

"I'll draw you a picture even you can understand," Captain Ed said grimly. "Here's the money to pay you off. There's a hundred seiners out there on the dock, and maybe five hundred more aboard their boats in the bay. I'm going to call every man jack of them in here. I'm going to explain the whole situation. Then I'm going to offer you this money, and I want them to hear you refuse to take it. Every good seiner gets in trouble once in a while, and its been the practice of the canneries to help them out in one form or another. And it's also worked the other way when the seiners have helped out the canneries at times. I want all these men to see the sort of deal they can expect if they ever come to you in trouble. Especially when there's six other canneries nearby they can go to and get a square deal."

"That ain't gonna do you any good."

"You think about it. How many fish will those seiners bring you next year when they see the kind of man you really are? This story will be well publicized over the whole Sound. Maybe next year we won't have a big run. We don't usually have two big runs in a row. A seiner can take his catch to any cannery he pleases, and he's going to help the cannery he likes. You figure to be liked, Frank?"

Brad watched the little cannery owner fight the battle with himself. He saw the desire to challenge Captain Ed tighten Karlson's small mouth and narrow his eyes. Then he saw the eyes slide toward the noisy group of fishermen on the dock, and he could guess what the little man was thinking. In a bad year those seiners could break him. He saw Karlson's shoulders slump, his eyes slide away from the window, and the tight line of his mouth loosen. Even before Karlson spoke, Brad knew that Captain Ed had won.

"All right," Karlson mumbled. "But you're breakin' your contract with me. I'm doin' this outa goodwill. Nothin' else."

"Of course," Captain Ed agreed.

Thirty minutes later they were outside on the dock, and Captain Ed held the mortgage for the *Annie B.* "Let's take it home and let Annie burn it."

"She'd like that." George stretched his huge arms above his head, "Well, another season gone. It started mighty rough but it turned out fine."

"Couldn't have been better," Captain Ed agreed. "Do you fellows want to go uptown for anything, or shall we head right out for home? I know Annie's been sitting on pins and needles, wondering how we've made out."

"Let's go home," George said. "Okay by you, Champ?"

"That's fine with me."

They went past the gang of fishermen, along the dock to the stairway, and were starting down, when a man hailed Captain Ed. Brad had seen Marshal Fred Thompson before. He was a lean, tough old man somewhere in his sixties, with a shock of snow-white hair blowing in the bay breeze. The first time Brad saw him he had looked for a star and a gun and belt studded with cartridges. But Marshal Thompson carried the star and gun in the pocket of an old brown canvas coat he always wore.

Captain Ed said, "Well, Fred, you'll have your town back all nice and quiet soon."

"I will that," the marshal agreed. "But I hate to see the season end and all you boys leave. It makes the town seem awful dead." He bent pale-blue eyes on Brad and asked, "Would you be Brad Nichols, boy?"

"Yes, sir," Brad said.

Thompson turned to Captain Ed. "There's a woman in my office who flew in from Anchorage less'n an hour ago.

She come all the way from Seattle to get the boy. Says she's his aunt. You and the boy better come to the office."

Brad's heart gave a great leap and seemed to stop dead. All the fear and dread of the past months rushed upon him, leaving him sick and numb. Down the dock he heard a man laugh cheerful and carefree. The gulls cried and quarreled over the offal chute. Below him a boat pulled out and pointed its nose toward the sea.

Then Captain Ed said quietly, "We'll go with you now, Fred."

"I'll wait aboard the boat." George's big hand gripped Brad's shoulder. His ponderous fist came up under Brad's chin and tilted it up. "Chin up, Champ. I'll see you soon." Then he went lightly down the steps.

Brad walked between Captain Ed and the marshal, and the sick feeling in the pit of his stomach grew and grew.

The front room of the marshal's home had served as his office for twenty years. The room was big and old-fashioned. It was furnished with a davenport, a number of straight-backed chairs, and an old battered desk and swivel chair.

A woman sat across the room in one of the straight chairs. She was wearing a dark suit and a high-necked blouse, and she sat very stiff and prim. Her hair was formed in a braid that was wound tightly around her head.

Marshal Thompson said, "Miss Haskin, this is Captain Ed Bishop and this is your nephew, Brad Nichols."

Captain Ed removed his cap, crossed the room, and shook hands with her. Brad, not knowing what else to do, followed. She held her hand out to him. He took it, and her grip was firm and strong. She looked at him soberly, as if measuring

178

him against something, and said in an even voice, "Bradley, I should have come long ago."

He said, "Yes, ma'am." So this was the Aunt Clara he'd been plotting against all these months, whom he'd been trying to avoid for so long. She looked a little like his mother, only bigger and thinner. And now that he was close he could see that her hair was tinged with gray and that her eyes were large and brown and steady. There was something about her that was harder than his mother. Maybe it was the straight lips pressed firmly together, the square set of her shoulders, or the ramrod-straight way she sat. She looked tough and uncompromising. She had always backed away from his mother and once from Gram. Brad felt she wouldn't back off now.

Captain Ed returned across the room and sat on the davenport. Brad followed and sat beside him.

Marshal Thompson sprawled his long length in the old swivel chair, scowled, and dug his fingers through his white hair. Finally he asked, "You have a good season?"

"Very good."

"How's the new boat?"

"Great. She's very seaworthy."

"Captain Bishop got a new seiner," the marshal explained to Aunt Clara. "She's one of the finest in the Sound."

Aunt Clara smiled faintly and said, "That's nice."

The marshal asked Brad, "How'd you like seining?"

"Fine," Brad said, and added for the benefit of Aunt Clara: "I'm going to have my own boat someday. Isn't that right, Captain Ed?"

Captain Ed rubbed his long jaw and glanced at Aunt Clara, "We did discuss it some."

"Marshal," Aunt Clara's precise voice cut in, "can we get on with our business? I've come a long way."

"Sure. Sure." Marshal Thompson scratched his head again and inched himself higher in the chair. "Guess we all know why we're here. Miss Haskin got Annie's letter telling about the boy, and she's come up to get him and take him back to live with her. Guess that's about it in a nutshell."

Aunt Clara nodded. "I appreciate what Captain and Mrs. Bishop have done for Bradley. But now I'll take over."

Captain Ed said to Aunt Clara, "I can understand your wanting to take Brad, but there are other things to be considered here."

"What are they, Captain?"

"Brad's no baby any more to be passed from hand to hand. He took the place of a man aboard the boat all season. Not because he had to, remember. He wanted to. And he did his job. On top of that, he's lived with us all winter and summer. We want to keep him and he wants to stay. He's a part of the family now."

"That right?" the marshal asked Brad.

"Yes," Brad said as emphatically as he could. "I want to stay with Captain Ed and George and Annie. And someday I'm going to have my own seiner."

Marshal Thompson looked at Aunt Clara.

"He's fifteen years old," Aunt Clara said. "He's just a boy. He's lived out on that little Glacier Island all his life. He doesn't know what he's saying or what he really wants."

"I know," Brad insisted. "I don't want to go to Seattle or anyplace else, ever!"

"Easy, son," Captain Ed soothed. "Fred"—he turned to

the marshal—"doesn't the fact Brad's been with us so long, that we want him, that he wants to stay, and that we can give him a good home count for something?"

"Course it does." Marshal Thompson hitched himself a little higher in the chair again, and glanced furtively at Aunt Clara. "It counts for plenty."

"But not enough," Aunt Clara said firmly. "In the eyes of the law Bradley is still a minor, in spite of his work this summer. I'm his only living relative, blood relative. And, Marshal, I, too, am perfectly capable of giving Bradley a good home. Besides, I can give him the benefit of the best schools, good care and guidance, and all the advantages of a big city. I talked with an attorney before coming North, and he assured me that what I am doing is not only legally right but morally just. If you doubt me, feel perfectly free to call in an attorney for an opinion. I'm sure there must be one in Orca City."

Marshal Thompson squirmed uncomfortably, scratched his head, and scowled at the desk top. "That won't be necessary," he said finally. He looked at Captain Ed and Brad and spread his big hands in a helpless gesture, "There you have it, Ed. She said it all. She can do everything for the boy you can, and more. According to the law, blood relation takes precedence over everything else. Even if I wanted to, I couldn't argue against that, and neither can you. I'm sorry, Ed. I was hoping we could work something out." He shook his head. "The boy goes with his aunt."

"Nothing doing!" Captain Ed's voice was harsh; his cheeks were flushed with anger. "I won't go for that!"

"Maybe I don't like it either," the marshal continued quietly, "but I haven't any choice. It's right and it's lawful."

181

"It may be lawful but it's not right," Captain Ed shot back. "What's right is that Brad don't want to go and we don't want him to. And he's not going, if I've got to fight it with every dime I've got."

"It'll take every dime, and more," the marshal said positively, "and you'll still lose. Believe me, Ed, Miss Haskin is on sure ground. I know it and you do, too."

"I made very sure of that before I came all this way," Aunt Clara said. "I don't want trouble, Captain, but Bradley is going with me. I think I know what's best for him."

"I doubt that."

Marshal Thompson's voice was final: "This's how it's got to be, Ed. So don't give me any trouble. It's tough enough on the boy as it is. Don't you make it worse by kicking up a fuss."

Brad held his breath and watched Captain Ed's stormy face. He knew his future for all time was being decided in Captain Ed's mind, and tension built in him like a tightening fist. Captain Ed looked at the marshal, then at Aunt Clara sitting calm and sure. He looked down at his big hands and pressed them together so tight his knuckles were white and muscles jumped in his thick wrists. Finally he leaned back with something like a sigh, and, not looking at Aunt Clara or Brad, asked in a curiously flat voice, "When do you want to leave?"

"Captain Ed!" Brad cried. "You can't! I won't go! I won't! This is my home. You know it is."

"I know it," Captain Ed agreed. "But I haven't any choice, son. We haven't any choice. I guess I've always known this's how it'd turn out, if it came right down to it. Annie's always known it, too. We always hoped it wouldn't come to this."

Brad was all set to argue further, to make a real fight of it, but the sick look on Captain Ed's face stopped him. If Captain Ed wouldn't fight, he was licked. The very thing he had dreaded, and fought and schemed against since the day his parents had drowned off Kodiak, had at last come to pass. Then Aunt Clara said in her matter-of-fact voice: "I want to leave in the morning. I understand that's the first plane I can get out of here. We'll stay at the hotel tonight."

"I've got clothes and things," Brad mumbled. "I want to say good-bye to Annie. And what about Mickie?"

"We'll get new clothes in Anchorage," Aunt Clara said.

"I can't leave Mickie."

"Your dog?" Aunt Clara shook her head. "It's best if you leave him here with Captain Bishop and we just go on. You're away now, Bradley. You can write Mrs. Bishop when we get home."

He was about to argue when Captain Ed put a hand on his arm. "She's right, son. This is the way Annie would want it, too. More good-byes just make it tougher. We'll take care of Mickie."

"All right," Brad agreed. "But I won't stay in any old hotel tonight. I'm staying aboard the *Annie B* with you and George." He was determined to have his way in this one thing, and was ready to fight everyone in the room for it.

Aunt Clara bit her lip and looked at Captain Ed. "Very well," she agreed, "if Captain Bishop will see that you're aboard the plane tomorrow morning."

183

"He'll be there." Captain Ed rose. He said good-bye to the marshal, and told Aunt Clara that they were all sorry to lose Brad and that he hoped everything worked out well for both her and Brad. As they started out, Aunt Clara reached for Brad's arm. For the first time her voice was not cold and impersonal. "I'm sorry, Bradley. I'm doing this for your sake. Someday you'll see it."

Brad jerked his arm away and followed Captain Ed outside. It was the only act of defiance he had left.

They were halfway through town before Brad gathered his wits, and remembered, "I forgot you wanted to leave for home right away."

"You're staying aboard the *Annie B* tonight," Captain Ed said grimly. "A few hours more getting home won't matter."

George looked at their faces when they entered the galley, then he leaned against the sink, folded his arms, and waited. They both sat down at the table, and finally Captain Ed told George what had happened. George nodded, and when Captain Ed finished he said, "It couldn't go any other way if she wanted him, Champ being a minor and all."

Brad looked out the open door at the bay, the wheeling gulls, and the sea stretching away to the distant snowy mountains. "She can't keep me forever. Someday I'll come back."

"We'll be right here waiting, Champ."

"With the new seiner tied to the dock all spick-and-span and ready to go," Captain Ed added.

"I'll be the crew." George smiled. "We'll make the whole Sound sit up and take notice when we run out a seine."

So they talked, and the time passed. Finally George got out

184

the pans and cooked supper, but none of them ate much. Afterward they sat on deck and watched the northern dusk come down. The gulls settled on piling ends, along the dock railing, and lined the cannery ridge. A light or two came on in the town. Boats continued to leave at irregular intervals, heading back over the long miles home.

"We might as well turn in," Captain Ed said finally. "You'll have to be up early, son."

They went below and rolled into their bunks. Brad lay staring into the dark, listening to the night come alive. Finally Captain Ed's voice said into the silence, "You awake, son?"

"Yes."

Captain Ed turned on his side, and Brad could see the pale shine of his long face. "I couldn't stop her," he said. "Your aunt's a very determined woman. I couldn't get rough with her the way George did with Karlson. When she wouldn't give in, the marshal had no choice but to side with her."

"I saw that."

"I think we've dreaded this time as much as you have. You're the closest to a son we've ever come."

"I feel that way, too."

"You being down there can't change that. George and I meant what we said, and Annie will, too. We'll all be right here waiting."

"I'll remember," Brad said.

"Good. I wanted you to know."

Silence settled into the compartment again. Brad heard George's deep even breathing, and after a long time he knew Captain Ed was asleep, too. His mind went back to Annie.

185

He thought of her iron will and determination, her gravelly, tough voice. He should have had Annie along at the marshal's office. Captain Ed had been handicapped from the first because he was a man. Annie would have given Aunt Clara a battle. Tough little Stampede Annie would have fought his aunt to a standstill. Nobody licked Annie when her fighting blood was up. She could be as vicious as the wolverine had been.

He lay still, held by a surprising thought. After a little while, he carefully slid his legs over the side of the bunk and sat up. Annie would back him up. She wouldn't give up the fight the way Captain Ed had. She was a woman, and it took a woman to fight a woman. Annie was tougher than the best day Aunt Clara had ever seen.

He could get to Annie. He remembered the winter day she had told him that the line of mountains they could see from the valley led straight to Orca City's main street. It was the sixty-mile trail she had taken every winter with her dog team to Orca City for supplies.

He remembered something else. In summer that was sixty of the toughest miles in the North: mosquitoes, brown bears, boggy marshes, brush, rockslides, and icy streams to cross. He remembered the bush pilot who had crashed and hiked out only thirty miles, but he'd been a sorry sight. He'd have to hike the full sixty. But he could do it.

He stood up carefully, picked up his clothes and shoes, and tiptoed into the galley. There he pulled on his shirt, pants, and socks. Then he stood there planning what he'd need. He'd need food. But he didn't dare move about opening drawers and making sandwiches for fear of waking one of the

186

men. The light rifle stood in a corner. He'd take that. He'd need it for protection, and he could kill his food as he went. He filled his pockets with matches, found half a box of shells, and took them all. Carrying the rifle and his shoes, he tiptoed outside, went over the rail, and lowered himself to the float.

When he reached the stairs he put on his shoes, went swiftly up to the dock, along it, and came into the town's one street.

The street was dark except for an occasional light. He went hurriedly along the boardwalk, ready at any moment to duck into the black holes between buildings should anyone appear. When he came to the far end of town, he stood in the dark at the end of the street and looked at the mountain rising sheer into the pale northern night. This was the first of many such mountains and ridges. He must follow very carefully along the base of them. Sixty miles away lay the valley, home, and Annie.

twelve

A hundred feet beyond the end of the street, Brad stopped and loaded the rifle.

It was rough traveling at night. He slipped often and fell as he tripped over roots, rocks, and limbs. But he had to travel all this first night. It was important to get as far from Orca City as possible in the shortest space of time. Captain Ed and George would be looking for him in a couple of hours, sooner if they woke and discovered him gone.

He kept up a steady pace for the first two or three hours. The dark silhouette of the mountain rose steeply above him and was an easy beacon in the pale northern night. He must keep it on his left, he told himself. He must keep all mountains on his left and follow this line of peaks and ridges. He stopped once to rest. He could see the faint shape of another peak stabbing the stars far ahead. That would be his next goal. He looked to the right. There were no mountains, and he was sure the flat, brushy tundra stretched away two or three miles to the sea.

Finally he left the mountain he'd been following. The land tipped down in a gentle running slope that led him into a valley where he entered a dense stand of timber. The trees closed in so tightly that only at long intervals could he see the night sky. Not once did he glimpse the mountain he was steering by. He stopped short and fixed the mountain's position firmly in his mind. He couldn't afford to get lost and lose hours wandering in circles. Annie had once told him how easy it was to become lost. "Keep in mind where you're going and where you've been. Don't wander along wool-gathering. Keep your wits about you."

He moved forward carefully, keeping Annie's advice in mind, holding the light rifle firmly in both hands. He had never been in dense timber before at night. It was an eerie, frighteningly unreal sensation. The actual going was not bad. There were no rockslides to detour around, no underbrush to fight, and the ground was fairly free of tripping roots and limbs.

It must have taken more than an hour to thread his way through the timber. When he at last emerged out the other side and looked up anxiously for the black bulk of the mountain he'd been following, there it was dead ahead.

As he sat down on a rock to rest, he knew a feeling of triumph. He'd hiked several miles without a landmark to guide him and had come out exactly where he wanted to. He wouldn't be so afraid of the next block of timber. And the worry that he might not be able to follow the line of peaks and ridges was now completely gone.

The night was spent, and he watched morning light spread thinly across the distant mountain slopes and seep downward into the black creases of the hills and valleys. The sky became blue, and the stars faded. Then the day came full blown.

He was tired and sleepy, but he knew he dared not rest yet. He rose and went on into a wide, flat valley. It looked like easy traveling from a distance. But the waist-high grass was thick and tough. Brad frightened up a mother duck and a dozen downy babies. The babies scattered through the deep grass, and disappeared while the mother fluttered down the tiny stream, trying to entice him away. A pair of Canada geese honked loudly in alarm, craned long necks, and watched nervously as he passed.

Brad hadn't progressed far when he realized he was in for real trouble. Mosquitoes boiled out of the grass at his feet and formed in a hungry cloud above his head. He tried to beat them off by slapping and frantically waving his free arm, but they swarmed over his face, hands, and across his back and shoulders, where their stinging drove through his thin summer shirt. He knew he could never stand this for the time it would take to cross the wide valley. He splashed to a low green bush, ripped off a half dozen well-leafed limbs, bunched them, and fanned them in a circle above his head. This drove off the bulk of the mosquitoes, but they followed him, milling in a ball as big as a barrel just above the swirling brush. Every few seconds a few dived in and got to him. These he could stand. But he had to get across the valley at top speed because he couldn't continue swirling the brush indefinitely.

It took several hours to cross the valley, and he'd been forced to stop a number of times to rest. He shifted the rifle and the brush from hand to hand frequently, but if he stopped for an instant the whole swarm was at him.

When Brad stumbled out of the valley onto solid ground, he was soaked and muddy from head to foot. He stumbled a hundred yards up into a boulder field and flopped down in the shade of a rock. Oddly, in this short distance from the valley floor there were no mosquitoes.

He lay for some minutes, flat on his back, resting. Then the torture of insect bites and a throat so dry he could not swallow got him up. He had to find clear, running water to wash the mosquito bites and get a drink. He'd been afraid to drink from the many small streams because the water seemed dead, and teemed with bugs. He was ravenously hungry, too. He'd have to keep a sharp lookout for a rabbit or a ptarmigan.

He crossed the boulder field, entered flat, brushy country, and soon came to a clear, fast-running stream. He stripped and plunged into the icy water and swam furiously for a few seconds. Then he stood waist-deep and washed as best he could. The cold was balm to his burning skin, and he stood it as long as possible, then waded ashore and dressed.

He caught a flash of red in the water a few feet off and discovered a shallow pool where a small school of salmon were cruising back and forth over the clear, pebbly bottom. They had all turned from silver to a violent red, and some had white splotches on their sides. They had spawned here and were now cruising over the eggs. They would continue to do so until they died. The violent red and white showed they were actually rotting to death. They were no longer fit to eat. If he could find one that had just come up from the ocean, he might be able to shoot it or snare it somehow. It

191

would be good eating. He searched along the stream for some distance, but he found no other salmon.

As he went on, his driving need now was for food. A half hour later he spotted a ptarmigan sitting on a bush. He dropped to his hands and knees and crept forward, taking advantage of every bush, grass clump, and rock. He was thankful the bird was not among the most wary. The ptarmigan was picking at half-ripe blueberries, and paid no attention until Brad was quite close. Then it raised its head and held perfectly still, studying him. The bullet took its head off neatly. He cleaned the bird, built a fire, and roasted it on a stick over the coals. He ate half, stuffed the remainder in his pockets, and went on.

Brad traveled along the rim of a valley, following the line of ridges and peaks until the heat of the afternoon. He'd been hiking since midnight. He must have come twelve or fifteen miles. He decided he was so far away now he couldn't easily be found. It was safe to take a good rest. He hunted up the shade of a large bush, propped the rifle carefully against a stone within easy reach, and flopped at full length. He was asleep almost immediately.

He slept longer than he'd planned, and when he awoke the sun was sliding toward a belt of trees. He began hiking again, eating the remainder of the ptarmigan as he went. The sleep had refreshed him; his stomach was reasonably full and his line of travel plainly visible. For the first time he felt fairly cheerful. He'd do another four or five miles before dark, then hunt for a place to hole up. From now on, he decided, he'd travel only in daylight.

He crossed two more swift-running streams, one almost

chest-deep, where he held the rifle above his head in one hand, the fistful of matches in the other to keep them dry.

The sun sank behind the trees, and shadows gathered and blackened the earth. He began searching for a spot to spend the night, and found it in a niche of rock a few feet off the ground. The rock was warm from the heat of the day, and soon his clothing dried. He slept with the precious rifle cradled in his arms.

The first gray streaks were lighting the sky when Brad was up and traveling again. He was ravenously hungry, and on the lookout for breakfast. He skirted the base of a hill and started out across a stretch of rolling tundra dotted with potholes, small pools of brackish water where the heavy rains had drained into low spots. The ground was soft around these stagnant pools, and he detoured around them until he came to a particularly large one that wandered between two low hills for several hundred yards. It was only six or eight feet across. No need to walk all that way around. He'd better save himself when he could. He ran and jumped across. He landed a good two feet beyond the water's edge, but to his horror he crashed right on through and went completely under into a black, terrifying world. He fought frantically to the surface, caught at the edge of the tundra, broke through, caught again, and slowly, inch by inch, eased himself on top, where he lay shivering with cold and shock. This stagnant pool was big, but the netlike tundra moss had grown almost completely over it. His weight, landing solidly, had broken through it.

He rolled over and began searching frantically. The rifle was gone. Then he remembered. As he went under he'd let go of it and grabbed for the edge of the tundra. He thought briefly of trying to dive for it, but the chill darkness terrified him. If he came up under the mat of tundra moss, he'd never break through to air. He'd drown.

He crawled away from the hole and stood up. He was sick at losing the rifle. Now he had no protection from wild animals or any other living thing that might threaten him in this wild stretch of country, and no sure way to get food. Then he remembered the matches, and carefully delved into his soaked pocket for them. They were wet and some of the heads were already falling off. He spread them carefully on the moss where the sun could dry them. He took the shells from his pocket and started to throw them away. They were of no use without the rifle. But somehow he couldn't part with them. He returned them to his pocket.

Brad watched the matches anxiously. When at last he felt they were dry enough, he tried lighting one. The head crumbled. He tried another and another. None was any good.

He looked at the useless matches, at the dark water hole on the bottom of which lay the rifle. There was nothing to stay here for. He rose and walked away.

The sun was high and hot when he came off the tundra and dropped down into another valley laced with a network of good-sized streams. He stopped at the first and drank his fill. When he rose to his hands and knees he saw salmon cruising along the bottom. They were bright silver. These salmon had recently come upstream from the sea, and would be good to eat. Maybe he could catch one with a loop made of his belt or find a shallow riffle where he could club one to death. But he had no matches, and he wondered if he could eat one raw. Before he could decide, he saw the brown bear.

It came out of brush on the opposite side of the creek, no more than fifty feet off, ambling slowly down the bank.

Brad scrambled backward from the edge of the stream and rose cautiously. The bear stopped at the water's edge and looked across at him with weak, piglike eyes. His black nose twitched as he reached for the boy's scent. He swung his big head and "whoofed" sharply. Then he walked into the creek to where it was several feet deep and sat down with his back against the fast-flowing current. A salmon swam into the eddy created by the bear's big body and hung there to rest. The animal plunged his head into the water and came up with the salmon wriggling in his jaws. He held it between his paws and leisurely began to eat.

Brad hurried away. He crossed a half-dozen streams in the valley, and none was less than waist deep. He saw a number of bears. Some were fishing; the rest were feeding on grass and roots on the valley floor. He detoured around them and avoided all brush patches where one might be napping in the shade. The line of peaks finally led him out of the valley and onto higher ground.

The water he'd drunk at the creek had helped his hunger only temporarily. He was ravenous again. He began searching for berry bushes as he traveled. He found a scattering of half-ripe blueberries, and stripped the bushes. The berries were very sour, and there weren't enough to take the edge from his hunger. He came on a likely spot and searched on hands and knees for strawberries, but there were none.

It was turning toward the pale of evening when he came

to the bank of a small stream. There on the opposite side squatted a small log cabin. He splashed eagerly across, lifted the latch, and shoved open the door. It was an abandoned trapper's or miner's cabin. He saw an old bunk, a small table, and a rusting Yukon stove in the center of the room. A pair of shelves was nailed to one log wall. A single rust-pitted can stood on one shelf. It looked like a can that might hold beans. With a nail, he punched a hole in the can and eagerly hacked out the top. One smell was enough to tell him it could not be eaten. Yet he tried. But he couldn't get the first bite down. He pushed the can away and stood looking at it. Suddenly he snatched it up, rushed outside, and hurled it savagely against a tree.

He remembered the stove and went back inside. If he could start a fire he'd find a salmon in the creek, and no matter how old and rotten it was he'd cook and eat it. If not a salmon, then a sucker, a trout—anything. He spent a good half hour looking for matches, but found none.

He remembered a picture he'd seen of an Indian starting a fire by spinning a stick between his palms until the friction ignited some pulverized bark dust. The powder from a rifle shell was better than bark dust. He found a stick and sharpened it, then whittled the lead from one of the shells and spilled the powder in a small pile on a flat board. He spun the stick until his hands ached, but he barely warmed the end of the stick. He finally gave up, went down to the creek, and again drank his fill of water. He returned and lay on the hard bunk. But gnawing hunger kept him awake most of the night.

He took a drink at the creek again the next morning, then

196

hiked off through a chill, misty dawn. This time the drink did not ease his pangs of hunger.

He began searching for berry bushes as he went. He crossed several streams, pausing on the bank of each to scan the pebbly bottom for spawning salmon. At the next stream he crossed, he spotted a few stragglers nosing along the bottom. Their color was still silvery.

He tried the bear's trick. He waded into the stream and stood waiting. But his body wasn't large enough to form an eddy where a salmon fighting its way upstream could rest. He tried stabbing his hand into the water to grab one, but they were much too quick for him. He tried until his legs became numb and he had to quit the stream. He wandered along the bank, searching for a shallow riffle where he could club one to death. He came, instead, to a long, deep section of creek, and here the stragglers were spawning. There were no salmon beyond this deep area, so he reluctantly left the stream.

He continued to cross streams at such regular intervals that for the next several hours his clothes never dried. Later he found a few blueberry bushes, and stopped to eat. Though the berries were less than half ripe, and very sour, he began stripping the bushes and cramming the fruit into his mouth. He rounded an alder bush and came face to face with a bear who was also eating berries.

For a little while boy and bear just looked at each other. Then the bear reared to his great heart-stopping height on hind legs, huge forepaws hanging loosely before him. He swung his great head right and left, sampling the slight breeze. It was the typical act of a brown bear who is annoyed, uncertain, or has found something his insatiable curiosity says needs investigating. Brad knew that the animal could see him and that the breeze carried his hated man scent straight to those twitching nostrils.

Brad backed off, hurriedly glancing about for some place to run. Several hundred feet off was a lone tree with low-hanging branches. He backed toward it. The bear dropped on all fours and came toward him. He had decided to investigate. Brad turned and ran for the tree. At every step he expected one of those great paws to smash him to earth or to feel the bear's teeth in his back. How he dived into the tree's protective branches and climbed so fast he never knew. When he finally stopped climbing and looked down, the bear was reared on hind legs against the trunk, forepaws upthrust, looking up at him. He growled ominously, and his huge claws ripped off great sections of bark. The tree was too big for the bear to push over and his body was too heavy to climb it. Ripping off the bark as high as he could reach and growling around the base was the most he could do. This he did for some time.

The sun was hot, and Brad was uncomfortably perched on a limb some twenty feet up. Apparently the bear became uncomfortable, too. He finally wandered back to the brush patch and began to eat berries. As Brad watched him strip the bushes, he could almost hear the satisfied smacking of the animal's lips. He almost tasted the juice bursting and filling his own parched mouth as the big teeth crunched down.

The bear was reared on hind legs against the trunk, forepaws upthrust, looking up at him.

After eating his fill, the bear stretched out for a nap in the shade of a bush.

Brad waited a few minutes more, then slowly, quietly crept down the tree, and tiptoed away. He kept his eyes open for bears after that, but he saw none, and found no more berry bushes.

His hunger had become a devouring ache that sapped his strength, and he stopped often to rest. It was at one of these times that he noticed his shoes. The soles didn't look right, and he inspected them. They were coming loose. Wading so many streams, hiking across rocky slopes and through mud had been too much for them. Brad knew these shoes had to last. Crossing those flinty inclines would be murder barefoot. From now on he'd have to carry his shoes when he waded streams and pushed through marshy valleys.

He followed the base of a mountain for some time, then crossed a barren shale slope where the going was slow and the sun beat down on him. He dropped into a fine flat, grassy valley. Only when he was into it did he realize it was another marshy mosquito haven, veined with a network of tiny streams and stagnant pools.

Brad removed his shoes, tied the laces together, and slung them around his neck. He hunted for a bush, broke off a handful of well-leafed limbs to whirl around his head, and went forward.

As before, the swarm of mosquitoes boiled above his head, and every few seconds a dozen or so got through the fan of leaves to sting. Barefoot was slower traveling. Some of the wide, flat grass-blades were sharp as knives, and he soon had slashes across both feet and ankles. After a good half mile of this, he was tempted to put his shoes on so he could make better time. But he dared not. He was going to need those shoes much more when he crossed another slope of shale.

When he finally stumbled out on the far side of the valley, both feet were bleeding. He'd fallen half a dozen times; his face was cut and his right hand was bleeding. Once again every exposed inch of skin was on fire with mosquito bites. This time he had to drag himself several hundred yards up the slope to escape the insects. Exhausted, he crawled into the shade of a bush and lay at full length. Again his mouth was dust-dry and his stomach was tied in knots of hunger.

He wondered how much longer he could go on. Doubts poured in upon him. People had died of starvation in these northern wilds, even in summer. About one more day without food and he would be through. Maybe he was lost anyway. During that first night when he'd hiked so long, maybe he'd got turned around somehow in the dense timber and picked out the wrong mountain range to follow. He could be heading in most any direction. He'd seen no gulls for two days now, so he couldn't be close to the coast. He'd always understood that the range Annie pointed out to him followed the coast. There should be gulls several miles inland. His shoes weren't going to cover many more miles before the soles fell off. And he'd taken about all the marshy bogs and mosquitoes he could.

Running back to Annie had been a crazy, spur-of-the-moment idea anyway. No matter how tough and uncompromising Annie was, George had called the turn that night early this spring when he'd said, "No fifteen-year-old boy can beat an adult in a case like this." Marshal Thompson had put it even stronger: "Blood relation takes precedence over everything else."

With Aunt Clara, Brad thought miserably, I wouldn't be half eaten by mosquitoes and I wouldn't be nearly starved. I've got to find something to eat soon.

He was so steeped in his own misery that at first he didn't hear the swift rush of sound. He became aware of the plane only when it burst over the slope like a yellow bullet and streaked across the valley at him so low it looked as if it were going to smash into the earth where he lay. The next instant it roared over him so near that he glimpsed the broad, scarred face of Big George peering down.

He leaped to his feet and rushed for the open. His bare foot struck a rock, and he sprawled headlong. He lifted his face up, a cry bursting from his lips: "George! Come back! Come back!"

But the plane fled on over the bulge of the earth, and disappeared. Not even the sound remained to tell it had passed this way.

thirteen

After the first shock of glimpsing George's broad face staring down over the side of the racing plane, Brad knew he was traveling in the right direction. They had guessed he was hiking back home, he reasoned, and George was searching the route with a bush pilot. The plane disappeared in exactly the direction he was going. A fresh rush of confidence and determination flooded over him. He'd make it! He shouldn't be too far from the head of the valley now. He remembered that this row of peaks took a definite turn at the valley and then lined out straight for Orca City. When he found that turn again, he'd be almost home. This was the third day, and he reasoned he'd hiked not less than twelve hours a day, not counting stops to rest. If he averaged a mile and a half an hour, that made eighteen miles a day. By tonight he should have traveled fifty-four miles. Call it fifty. Annie had said it was sixty miles to Orca City, so he should be no more than ten miles from home. Most of it was behind him now, and the miles ahead wouldn't be any tougher than those he'd already come. He could certainly make the rest. But he had to have something to eat. He had to have food.

He found it an hour later in the least promising spot. He was crossing an almost barren stretch of rocky slope when he glanced down and discovered he was walking over strawberries. He dropped to his hands and knees and began picking and eating ravenously. The berries were small and so overripe they were dry and almost tasteless. But they were food.

Brad spent almost an hour crawling about on the sun-drenched slope, eating his fill. When he finally rose and went on, the terrible hunger pangs had been eased somewhat and he felt stronger. Again he found a stream, stripped off his clothes, and waded waist-deep and washed his mosquito-bitten upper body. This time it didn't seem to help much. He guessed bites must be piling on top of bites.

He dressed again and went out across a flat tundra dotted with brush patches and an occasional stream. The day was fading and shadows were stretched across the tundra when he found a patch of still-green blueberries. They were very sour, but he ate them, and then drank at the next creek he crossed. Darkness closed in fast, and he began to hunt for a place to stop for the night. He waded another stream. A few feet above the water, on the lip of the bank, he found a cavelike depression in the loose rock at the base of a downed tree. It looked as if it might have been hollowed out by some big animal. It would be an ideal winter den for a brownie. But a bear or any other big creature that might sleep there tonight would already be in it. He crawled in, moved the rocks about for comfort, and lay down.

But there was to be no sleep for him this night. Wherever mosquitoes had got to him, his skin was on fire. Finally he crawled out, went to the creek, and washed again. Because the spots across his back and shoulders were impossible to reach, he soaked the tail of his shirt and spread it across his back and shoulders. That helped. He continued until the chill of the night and the water got to him and his teeth began to chatter.

He had barely returned to his nest under the downed tree and become comfortable when the cramps began. They kept him doubled up and squirming miserably most of the night. When they finally subsided, he lay shivering, too cold to sleep. So the short night passed, and dawn found him more tired than he'd ever been. For the first time he dreaded to start the day. But he crawled out, returned to the creek, had his morning drink, and again washed himself. The itching and burning were not so bad, but they still made him unconsciously scratch and twist in a search for comfort.

He was hungry, but the thought of eating dried-up strawberries or green blueberries was nauseating.

Leaving the creek, he crossed onto high ground where he stopped and studied the line of ridges and peaks he'd been following. They ran as straight as a gun barrel. Once again he tried to estimate the distance to the valley and home. But, as always, his judgment was confused by stops for rest and by marshy crossings and slopes that had slowed his progress. He hoped only that it was not too far.

For a time he passed over rough, rocky terrain; then the way led through patches of alder and scrub spruce. He crossed another marshy valley with his shoes again slung around his neck. And again he fought the ever-present mosquitoes and was cut on face, hands, and feet by the knife-sharp grass-blades.

Near the middle of the forenoon he began climbing a steeply rising slope, finally emerging on high, bare ground that gave him a good look at the surrounding country laid out beneath him. His heart almost stopped, then began to race furiously. There, less than an hour's hike over fairly easy ground, the range of peaks and ridges he'd been following took a sudden, dramatic turn toward the unseen coast. And far off, but clearly visible, lay the deep gouge of a large valley. He was approaching from the tundra side, and he could see the rolling, tumbled hills, the slash of the valley, and a series of snow-covered peaks that stretched away to disappear far inland. At this distance he couldn't be sure, but the lay of the land was right. An hour's fast hiking would bring him close enough to tell.

He forgot that he was hungry, that he was tired and had meant to rest, and that his back, face, and hands were on fire again from the bout with mosquitoes. He went down the slope at a run, and he continued running until the knife-sharp ache in his lungs told him he'd have to slow down.

Finally, from the rolling bread-loaf hills he looked down into the valley. There was the stream he knew so well wandering up its center, the various patches of brush, the sharp-cut ravine slicing into the hills. Up there, near the head of the valley, he had killed Old Toughy, and farther on, just beyond that turn, he had fought it out with the wolverine. This was his valley. He knew every square foot of it. He'd made it! He wanted to shout and laugh and run. But then he remembered he still had to deal with his aunt, and once again he was grim.

He dropped down onto the valley floor and came to the stream. He turned down the stream toward the sea and the mouth of the valley. Never had it looked so beautiful, so peaceful. A breeze funneled up the valley, cool, fresh, and heavy with the bite of the sea. Crows called as they passed overhead, and jays quarreled in the thicket. Gulls cruised endlessly over the stream or walked along the shore searching for the remains of dead salmon. A mother duck uttered a burst of alarm, and the drake stood in plain sight, green head high, turning slowly to watch his passing.

Then he broke out of the mouth of the valley and looked down the slope to the cabin. Smoked drifted lazily from the chimney. Beyond the cabin the sea was flat and calm, and he could see the white shape of the *Annie B* tied to the little dock.

He came down the slope at a stumbling run, and when he neared the cabin some sixth sense or sound warned Mickie. The dog tore out of the open kitchen door and rushed at Brad, barking at the top of his lungs. The next instant Brad was on his knees, had both arms around Mickie's neck and his face buried in the dog's thick fur. Mickie was whining and trying to twist his big head around to lick the boy's face.

Then Brad looked up and slowly rose, one hand twisted in Mickie's fur. Captain Ed, George, Aunt Clara, and Annie had come out the kitchen door. As he looked at each of them, his eyes sought Annie last. He said the only thing that came to his mind. He said it straight to Annie: "I had to come home.

I just had to." And with the words the strength seemed to leave him, the fierce desire that had sustained and driven him for endless hours and over tortuous miles was burned out. Exhaustion washed over him in a deepening wave.

It was George who moved. The big man was accustomed to acting in emergencies. He had an arm around Brad and was smiling down at him. His voice was gentle and understanding. "Champ, we're glad to have you back. Welcome home."

Then Annie had him, gruff, tough little Annie was leading him into the kitchen. He noticed, vaguely, that she was not wearing the sling, and he could see her arm was no longer bandaged. She had him in a chair, and her eagle-sharp eyes were poring over him. The roughness in her voice had everyone scurrying to do her bidding. "How long's it been since you ate?" And before he could answer, "Clara, open a can of that tomato juice on the shelf behind you and pour him a big glass. "Brad, get that shirt off and we'll take care of those mosquito bites. Ed, get the bottle of lotion off the dresser. George, go out to the freeze room and get the biggest, thickest steak you can find."

Even Mickie joined in. All the activity excited him, and he dodged about among the flying legs and finally reared up with his front paws on Brad's lap to attract his attention.

Annie pulled him down gently and patted his head. "I know," she said. "We're all glad he's back safe. Now you run outside and chase your tail. Just keep out from underfoot."

Mickie slunk into a corner, out of the line of traffic, and lay down, but his eyes never left Brad.

Brad's shirt was off and Annie was inspecting his back

209

when Captain Ed returned and handed her the bottle of lotion. Brad said: "I lost the rifle. I'm sorry."

"What's a little old rifle?" and Captain Ed smiled.

"I fell into a deep hole on the tundra and grabbed to keep from going under, and lost it."

Captain Ed squeezed his arm. "It was only a gun. We can buy another. Forget it, son."

As Aunt Clara put the glass of tomato juice before him, their glances met briefly. He saw that her brown eyes were liquid-soft with emotion. She said gently, "Drink it slowly, Brad. Sip it."

"That's right." Annie spilled lotion into her palm and began spreading it across his shoulders and back. "Your stomach's got to start working again."

The itching and burning began to leave, and wonderful coolness came to his back.

George returned with a huge steak, and Annie said, "Clara, how're you with steak?"

"How do you want it?" Aunt Clara shot back.

"Medium rare with plenty of juice."

"Medium rare it'll be. George, get me some more wood, and where's the pressure cooker? Potatoes will go fine with this steak."

By the time the steak and potatoes were ready, Brad's back, shoulders, arms, and face had been covered with lotion and he had finished the tomato juice. When he started to cut into the steak, Annie warned: "Take it easy. No gobbling. Take little bites and chew it good or you'll get sick."

This was the first good food he'd had in four days, and it

took all his will power to refrain from digging in and bolting it down. He thought he'd never get enough. While he ate, all four of them told him what had happened since the night he'd run away from the *Annie B.*

"I must have woke up a couple of hours after you'd gone," Captain Ed said. "At first I thought you'd just gone outside for a little. When you didn't come back I woke George and we began looking. We found the rifle and shells gone, and then we knew you'd taken off for someplace. We spent the first day hunting around town, talking with people and asking if anyone had seen you.

"The second day George remembered a couple of deserted miners' cabins a few miles out of town, and we hiked out there to check. We figured maybe you'd gone there to hide out and wait for your aunt to leave. Then we came up with the idea that maybe you'd caught a ride with some seiner heading back to the States and had returned to your old home on Glacier Island. That was your aunt's idea. George had another one."

George nodded. "I thought you might have headed back for Annie and Mickie and that was why you'd taken the rifle. So we split up. The Skipper and your Aunt Clara went to Glacier Island in the *Annie B.* I flew over the trail Annie used to take with the dog team. But I didn't see you, so I met the *Annie B* at Glacier Island and we all came here to talk with Annie."

"You flew right over me," Brad said. "I saw you looking down. But it happened so quick I couldn't move."

Annie said: "George and Ed were just getting ready to

211

start out backtracking toward Orca City when you showed up. If we hadn't found you today, by tomorrow we'd have had the marshal and half Orca City out searching for you."

"I sure caused a lot of trouble. I didn't think." He looked at Annie sitting there smiling at him. "I came home to talk to you. I had to talk to you."

"You finish your dinner."

He laid down his fork and pushed back the chair. "I'm full. I can't eat another bite. I want to talk to you now, Annie."

"Not now. You're going to get some sleep. You look like you haven't had a night's sleep since you left the *Annie B.* When you wake up we'll talk. We'll all talk."

"But, Annie—"

"We'll talk later. There's plenty of time. Now you march in there and go to bed."

He grinned. It was wonderful to have that gravelly voice ordering him around again. He went into the front room and flopped at full length on his cot. Mickie came in and curled up on the floor at his head. Brad reached down to rub the dog's sharp ears and twist his fingers in the thick fur. That was the last he remembered.

He awoke several hours later, and Mickie was still there. Brad lay staring at the ceiling, and thought how good it was to be home and how bossy Annie was. He thought of Aunt Clara in Annie's kitchen, pouring him tomato juice, frying his steak. She acted like one of the family, he thought, surprised, and she was being treated like one. He could think of only one reason for this change in her. She was trying to get on the good side of Annie, Captain Ed, and George so they'd be on her side when it came to forcing him to go back with her. He sat up and pulled on his shoes. He had to talk to Annie right now.

He was lacing his shoes when the door opened and Aunt Clara came in. She sat down in a chair near the cot and said: "You look like you had a good sleep. How do you feel?"

"Fine." He started to rise. "I've got to see Annie."

She put out a hand and stopped him. "Brad, I think we should have a talk."

"All right." His guard was up. "After I talk to Annie."

"Now, Brad! This won't take long." When he hesitated, half risen, she smiled and added, "Maybe afterward you won't have to talk to Annie."

He sank back on the cot and waited warily.

Mickie looked up at her. She leaned over and patted his head. Mickie grinned and pounded his tail on the floor.

She's even got him on her side, Brad thought, and was angry that Mickie had been taken in. Now she's going to try to win me over. He gripped the edge of the cot with both hands and set his mind firmly on refusal. He realized he was seeing a different Aunt Clara from the one he'd met in the marshal's office. Her hair still circled her head in the same tight braid and she sat very straight in the chair and she was dressed in the same plain blue suit. But she'd discarded the jacket, and her sleeves were rolled up, softening her appearance. But mostly he felt that her ramrod stiffness was gone. Her smile was soft, and the tough, uncompromising air was lacking. He remembered his mother had once said: "Clara's smart. She figures things out. She was always a jump ahead of me." He guessed she was being smart now. She's trying to get on the good side of me, he thought, so I'll give in easy. She's putting on an act.

"I've been teaching boys and girls about your age a long time," Aunt Clara began. "I know pretty well how they think and why they do things. I know why you came all this terrible distance home to Annie, and I don't blame you. Maybe I'd have done the same. I made a very bad start in the marshal's office. You see, I thought I was in for a battle with some—some rough frontier characters, and I was all primed for a knock-down, drag-out fight.

"Then I joined Captain Ed and George the morning you left, and learned the kind of people they really are. They were worried sick, and doing everything to find you. I felt even worse because I knew my attitude had caused you to run away. So the three of us worried and worked and hoped together.

"When we arrived here, Annie immediately began planning how the men would start out hunting you. She knew you were coming home. Annie's grand. In an hour I felt like I'd known her for years."

Brad felt his resentment slipping away, and reminded himself sternly that this was part of her act. He had to stay tough. "They made me feel at home from the first," he said. "They made me part of the family. And this is where I want to stay. This is where I'm going to stay—for always," he said stubbornly.

Aunt Clara nodded. "That's what I've been trying to put over. I understand completely. I know how much these people mean to you and how much you mean to them. I understand your love for this country. I've been here only four days, but I'd like to stay longer." She looked at her hands folded tightly in her lap, and spoke slowly, as if she dreaded each word: "That's why I'm not going to try to make you go back with me."

"You're not?" he asked suspiciously.

She shook her head, her brown eyes meeting his. "I thought I was coming up here to get a child who'd feel lost and needed help desperately. I learn you're no child and you're getting along fine. You're not like the young people I've worked with. If I forced you to come with me, it would be an unhappy experience for both of us. I'd like you to come, but only if you decide you want to. A big city has a lot to offer a boy like you. You'd see it, once you were there. There's a lot to be learned and to experience. Why, there's a whole world down there you know nothing about. You should dip into it, 'try it on for size,' so to speak. I'd like to help you discover it." She brushed at her skirt, then added: "That's all I wanted to say. Captain Ed and George are taking me back to Orca City tonight so I can catch the plane in the morning. I've been gone longer now than I'd planned. I'd like to have you go back with me. But it's your decision. Will you think it over?"

He said nothing.

She rose to leave, and then smiled down at him. The smile was like his mother's. "You know, you and I are part of a family, too, a real blood-relation family. And we're the last of it. It would be nice if we could stick together just a little."

After she'd gone he sat there and thought about her and the things she'd said. It hadn't been an act. This was the real Aunt Clara. Then he realized that all his resentment, his

215

desire to oppose her was gone. The thought frightened him. He had to talk to Annie. He needed to feel her strength and stubbornness. He wanted to hear that deep voice rock-solid with determination. With Mickie beside him he went into the kitchen and found Annie alone, peeling potatoes. "Where's everybody?" he asked.

"George and Ed are down at the boat. Clara's out looking around somewhere."

Brad made a restless turn around the kitchen. He looked out the window, glanced up at the big rifle, and thought briefly of its thundering voice and smashing power.

"How're the mosquito bites?"

"I don't feel anything."

"Good. You hungry? There's a little steak left. I can make you a sandwich."

"I'm not hungry." He leaned against the table. "Annie, she says I don't have to go back with her. I can stay?"

"I see."

"Is that all right with you and Captain Ed and George?"

"Is that what you want?"

"It's what I want."

"Then it's fine with us. You should know that."

He waited for Annie to say more, and was vaguely disappointed that she didn't. She wasn't helping at all. Finally he observed, "She's not like I thought she'd be."

"She's fine." Annie didn't look up from her peeling. "She came in, shucked off her coat, and pitched in like an old-timer."

Mickie sat down beside him and looked up. Brad scratched the dog's ears, frowning. Things weren't going as he'd expected with Annie, and he was at a loss. "I lied to you about her," he admitted finally. "She's always been interested in me. She helped out with books and laying out studies for me. I know Mom was glad for her help."

"After I met her, I figured that's how it was."

"I didn't want to leave," he said defensively. "I didn't know any other way."

Annie nodded, and continued peeling potatoes. "Find me the pressure cooker. Clara put it someplace."

He found the pressure cooker among the frying pans and stood watching her slice the potatoes in half. His thinking had taken an odd turn and he couldn't seem to stop it. "She is my aunt. My real aunt. I'm all she's got."

"And she's your only blood relative. You've discovered you could like her."

"I guess so." The thought surprised him. "But it's not just that."

"Blood relation," Annie said again.

"Annie," he burst out, "what'll I do?"

Annie laid down the knife, and turned. Her bright blue eyes dug into him. She folded her hands behind her back, squared her shoulders, and her small chin came up. Brad recognized the signs and knew that now he'd hear it. He'd hear that gravelly, tough, uncompromising voice say the things he'd traveled miles and almost starved and drowned to hear. This was the help he'd come for.

"It's your decision," Annie said then, and her voice had never sounded tougher. "Make it!"

"But, Annie!" he was shocked. "This is important!"

"You've been making important decisions ever since you

came here," Annie said flatly. "It was you decided to take a man's place and go seining this spring, and you fought me tooth and nail till I gave in. You decided to stay and help me with the berries and things. You made the decision to kill Old Toughy. You took over the house and canned the berries and cut wood and took care of me as good as any nurse could. You decided to make that sixty-mile hike back here when you knew how tough it'd be. How you came out looking so good, I'll never know. But anybody who can make all the decisions you have the past months can make this one, too."

Her words had scattered his thoughts in utter confusion. He threw the only argument at her he had left: "You said yourself I was too young to make an important decision. And what could be more important than this?"

"Years don't count for much," Annie answered promptly. "Like I told you. It's what's in here." She tapped her chest. "You've got pretty big in here this spring and summer. Big enough to decide what's best for you without any help from anybody. If you figure this out yourself, you'll stick with it. If we try to force something on you, you might run away from it like you just did. So put on your thinking cap and get busy. We'll all go by what you decide."

She went back to work on the potatoes, and he realized she had said all she was going to. He went to stand in the doorway for a time. Mickie joined him, and they walked out into the yard and started wandering up the slope. He walked all the way to the mouth of the valley, and Mickie stayed close beside him.

He sat on the stump and looked at the sunlit valley, and remembered. He remembered the winter trapping, the biting

218

cold, sitting on a log eating a sandwich and drinking chocolate with Annie, and feeling the utter silence with the vast
mountains leaning over them. He remembered the two
wolves chasing the rabbit, and how he'd killed the wolverine.
He remembered how spring had come to the valley, the
return of the ducks and geese and the host of small animals
that came from under the snow and out of dens to people the
valley. He remembered Annie sitting on the ground, bloody
and crying, and clinging to Mickie. He vividly remembered
his and Mickie's hunt for Old Toughy and the bear's final
charge down the bank into the creek after him.

Mickie reared against him. He put his arms around the
dog's neck and said, "We had some good times, didn't we?"
Mickie licked his face, and whined.

He looked down the slope, remembering how the cabin's
light spilled warm and inviting across the snow as they
returned each night from the trap line, tired and hungry and
laden with fur, and how Mickie came lunging up the slope,
setting the stillness ringing with his welcome. He thought of
the close companionship in the warm cabin, the good talk,
and the fun around the kitchen table after the dishes were
done.

He glimpsed a spot of white down there. Aunt Clara was
walking on the beach. He thought about her. He tried to do
it impersonally, but could not. She was Mom's sister. The
more he thought of that, the more important it seemed.
Annie had said, "You've discovered you could like her." And
Annie was right. Aunt Clara had sounded lonely when she'd
said they were the last of the family. He understood that
lonely feeling. He thought of the things she had done for

219

him over the years, the letters of advice to his mother, the books she had sent. She'd come two thousand miles for a boy she'd never seen. What she had said an hour ago was true.

All this he weighed against his desire to stay, against George, Captain Ed and Annie, and his love for the valley. He was surprised how calmly he could think about it. "You should be bawling your head off," he told himself. "You should be fighting mad, mad at Annie for throwing you over, mad at the marshal, mad at Captain Ed for giving up so easily, at George because he's so big and does nothing to help. Especially you should be mad at your aunt for coming up here and meddling in your life." Instead, he felt disappointed and heartsick.

He sat there a long time with his arms around Mickie. When he finally slid off the stump and started slowly back down the slope to the cabin, he had made up his mind.

They were at the table, about to eat a quick lunch, when he and Mickie entered. Brad went straight to his aunt and said, "Aunt Clara, I'm going with you."

Her eyes were wide. She put out a hand to touch him, and said, "Brad! oh, Brad!" Her voice broke and she looked away.

Brad turned to Annie. "I can't leave Mickie behind. We've been together too long. We—we've done too many things together. I'd be lonesome and so would he. I've got to take him with me."

Annie nodded and looked down at her plate.

Aunt Clara said: "Of course we'll take Mickie. I know how much he means to you."

Brad looked at Captain Ed. "You said I'd get a share for working on the boat. I want you to keep it. Buy something for the *Annie B* or—or something." He stopped. There was so much he wanted to say, and he didn't even know how to begin. He finished lamely, "I'll get my things ready."

Annie said gruffly, "They're all packed in George's suitcase."

"You knew I'd go?"

"I knew. Now sit down and eat. We've got something to say, too. Clara!"

Aunt Clara shook her head. "You tell him."

"We've been doing some thinking, too. You've got a couple of thousand dollars coming for your share of the catch. It'll be put in the bank in your name, and you can draw on it any time you like. Also, it'll give you enough money so you can come back here after school's out next spring. That's your Aunt Clara's idea. You can go to school and stay down in Seattle all during the school year. In the spring you can hop a plane, come home, and go fishing all summer and see the rest of us. In the fall you can fly back again. How do you like the idea?"

"You mean it? You really mean it?"

"Why not?" George smiled. "Thousands of others come north every year to fish, then go back. You did fine this year, and we need a pickup man every season. No sense spreading that money around when we can keep it in the family."

"It's wonderful," Brad said. "It's just wonderful."

"Frankly," Captain Ed added, "we don't see much sense letting you lie around all vacation, getting fat and soft."

Annie nodded. "We figure to work the socks off you every summer. Now, will you sit down and eat and quit hopping around like a grasshopper in a frying pan?"

221

From then on the kitchen was noisy, as it always was at mealtime. Aunt Clara joined in, but her eyes kept straying to Brad, and they were bright and happy, the way his mother's used to be.

Afterward they all trooped down to the little dock. Annie walked close beside Brad, her fingers twisted in Mickie's thick fur. Aunt Clara said good-bye to Annie, and went hurriedly aboard and into the galley.

Annie bent and held Mickie's big head between her hands and put her face against his forehead. "But for you I wouldn't be here. I'll never forget that," she said gruffly. "You be a good dog and take care of Brad and don't get in any trouble with those city dogs."

Mickie waved his tail and lifted his lips in a grin.

Annie gripped Brad's shoulders in both small hands and looked at him. Once again he was amazed at her strength. "You be good down there! And if you get homesick, just remember you'll be back again in a few months. And don't get run over by any of those crazy autos and taxicabs." She shook his shoulders, her small face all twisted up, and her voice sounded deeper, more gravelly than ever. "You be mighty careful," she warned almost angrily. "Hear?"

"I will," he said. "You too. And you look out for stray brownies, and don't trap this winter. We don't need it."

The *Annie B*'s motor kicked over and began to throb. Annie brushed a hand quickly across her eyes. Abruptly she pulled his head down and kissed him. "Go on, the both of you!" She shoved him toward the boat. "They're ready."

Brad said, "Come on, Mickie," and jumped aboard.

The *Annie B* pulled away from the dock and headed out

222

to sea. Aunt Clara, George, and Captain Ed were inside. Brad stood on the turntable in the stern, with Mickie beside him.

Annie shouted across the widening water, "You write every week or you'll be mighty sorry next spring!"

"I'll write," he shouted back.

Mickie realized Annie wasn't coming, and began to bark anxiously. Brad reached down and patted his head reassuringly. The dock and Annie's thin little figure grew smaller. Brad's eyes filled, and he shook his head angrily. When next he could see, Annie, the dock, and even the cabin squatting on the bank were gone. Only the towering snow-capped mountains remained.